The Bill 2

Also available from Thames Methuen

The Bill

The Bill 2

JOHN BURKE

Thames Methuen

THE BILL 2

First published in Great Britain 1987
by Methuen London Ltd
11 New Fetter Lane, London EC4P 4EE
in association with
Thames Television International Ltd
149 Tottenham Court Road, London W1P 9LL

Printed and bound in Great Britain
by Richard Clay Ltd, Bungay, Suffolk

British Library Cataloguing in Publication Data

Burke, John, *1922–*
The bill 2.
I. Title
823'.914 [F] PR6003.U54

ISBN 0–423–02240–7
ISBN 0–423–02160–5 Pbk

One

Word had come down from on high that the newcomer was to get no special treatment. At the same time they were to go easy on him, and if there was any sign of discrimination there would be trouble. The instructions were as devious as so many others issued by Chief Superintendent Brownlow: no matter which way his subordinates got it wrong, he would have covered himself.

This was PC Abel Lyttleton's third posting in three and a half years. He seemed to have had a bit of a problem settling down. Of course everyone appreciated that it was not easy, being a minority within a minority, as it were. Or at least, a lot of people appreciated it. There would always be one or two who didn't care for the colour of that sort of minority. But, stressed the chief super, if he found Lyttleton being subjected to any form of internal racial bigotry then he would have the offenders out of Sun Hill in a flash. Everybody in the building had better understand the score. This station was going to succeed where the others had failed.

Sun Hill nick had acquired its first black police constable.

The day of his arrival was not a particularly auspicious one for a newcomer. Electricians were rewiring the building and a new telephone switchboard was waiting to be connected. The VDU had gone blank. Lights in the front office came on for ten minutes, went off for fifteen. Even when there was a temporary restoration of current this seemed to be mainly for the benefit of a man with a power drill intent on making one hell of a row and a lot of dust on his way through the ceiling. Upstairs Sergeant Roach in CID was bellowed at by his detective inspector. Downstairs Sergeant Cryer did his own share of bellowing at the electricians until there was a serious danger of them all walking out on strike. And all the time, outside, the various villains of Wapping went about their business only too happy that lights, computers and, in particular, the recharge rack for the Old Bill's personal radios should malfunction or pack up altogether.

Sergeant Cryer treated himself to a short recuperative spell by giving PC Lyttleton a conducted tour of the main building. It was interesting to see it through fresh eyes. Each time he found a new recruit on his hands he found also a new perspective on familiar surroundings. Every day he must have gone in and out of that door to the yard and garages at least a dozen times. Today he noticed its refusal to shut: always an inch open this way or that, creaking to and fro in a conflict of draughts. There was an oddly dry, tangy smell in the corridor, and what looked like a layer of fine dust on the stairs to the first floor – only it wasn't dust, but the worn texture of the concrete. The impersonal bleakness of the interview rooms made them suddenly as grim to Cryer as they must be to so many reluctant visitors. He glanced at Lyttleton, whose expression gave nothing away. He was two inches taller than the sergeant and held himself with a stiff dignity, yet managed to be attentive and deferential without making too much of a thing of it, looking and listening and nodding but offering no opinion of his own.

It was a relief to take him up to the comparative brightness of the canteen and hand him over to the colleagues he would have to work with. Half a dozen of them were at a corner table. Rattling off introductions, Cryer wondered what Lyttleton would make of them; and what they would make of him.

The two girls, WPCs Ackland and Martella, smiled a welcome. Jimmy Carver half got up and said, 'How d'you do, mate.' Taffy Edwards and Yorkie Smith edged their chairs aside to make room.

Pete Muswell edged his chair a few inches as well – as far towards the end of the table as he could get it, his expression making no secret of what he thought of a black face. Cryer said, 'That one feeding his face along there is Pete Muswell.' Muswell left his food half finished, got up, and went out.

Lyttleton nodded. His face was as impassive as the sergeant's. 'One out of six ain't bad.'

No internal racial bigotry, right? But no special treatment. Cryer went off and left them to it. It was not going to be easy. Sooner or later there would have to be decisions: routine decisions in the case of most young officers, but not simple routine in this case. Not when you had to work out duty rosters and know that sooner or later Muswell and Lyttleton would have to be sent out on patrol together.

Bob Cryer turned his attention back to the problems of live wires and dead light bulbs.

There was a bang which made an electrician drop his screwdriver. Instinctively Cryer ducked. There had already been one sputtering explosion and a shower of sparks this morning. Any minute now he was ready for a chunk of ceiling to come crashing down.

The crash proved to come from the door at the foot of the stairs. Detective Sergeant Roach came storming through, followed by an apprehensive Mike Dashwood.

'Just the man I want to see,' said Cryer.

'Not now, Bob,' Roach growled.

DC Dashwood scuttled off along the corridor to the yard, intent on reaching the car before anything else fizzed off around his earholes.

'You know the power's going off again?' Cryer warned.

Roach glowered. 'Not upstairs it's not.'

'I'm telling you. They're turning off the electricity altogether for about half an hour.'

'As far as I'm concerned they can turn it off forever.'

Cryer steered him away from the greedy ears of front office staff towards the corridor. 'You sound pissed off. What's up?'

'I'll give you one guess.'

'Not His Nibs again?'

'I can think of a better name for him than that.' Roach's cheeks were mottled with rage. 'Listen, I promise you, I'll lose my pension over him. One of these days I'm just gonna lose my rag and slap one right on his bloody jaw.'

'Hey now, hold on. Hold on.' Cryer glanced aside as PC Smith started upstairs. 'Yorkie, on your way tell 'em the power's going off for another half hour, will you?'

'Right, sarge.' Smith glanced inquisitively at Roach, caught the blaze of the DS's eyes, and hastily went on up the steps two at a time.

'I promise you I will, Bob.' Roach had lowered his voice but it was as fierce as ever. 'I mean, he's bloody impossible.'

'Look, Ted, if the super thinks he's good enough to let him get away with it – '

'The super? All he's interested in is a quiet life and keeping his eyes on the next rung for promotion.'

'All right, I know. And you know about Roy and what he's been going through. Give him time. He'll come to terms with it.'

'Come to terms? He's had three months, for God's sake. He's not the first policeman ever to have been divorced, you know.'

No, thought Cryer, but for Detective Inspector Galloway anything, big or little, that went wrong was a first time. Any setback was a personal affront. And this one was very personal. You didn't get over fifteen years of marriage in just three months.

He said soothingly: 'Now leave it, right?'

Ted Roach, clearly unsoothed, pursued Dashwood out into the yard. Cryer sighed. Somebody today was going to suffer. A lot of people, maybe. Galloway was suffering, so that had to be passed on to his DS; and Roach would take it out on his subordinate Dashwood . . . and what poor victim was going to be at the final receiving end of all this aggro? Cryer could only hope it was a really deserving villain rather than a helpless innocent. He comforted himself with the thought that you didn't get many helpless innocents around Wapping.

Back in the front office turmoil, he stared up at the electrician balancing on a ladder. 'We've got to have that recharger working. It's top priority.'

'Can't work miracles, chief.'

Galloway stamped across the office. 'Bob, I'm off out for an hour. Roach and Dashwood are bringing in a Danny Plummer. Put him in a cell till I get back.'

'Is he a sticker, or what?'

'No, just a questioning.'

'Well, what if he . . .'

Cryer's voice trailed away. When it came to a matter of questioning, there were a couple of practical questions he would have liked answered himself before shoving someone into a cell. But it was too late. Galloway had already rampaged off into the outside world. Clearly it was going to get even rougher for somebody out there.

Cryer took a pace towards one of the filing cabinets, trapped his foot in a cable snaking its way across the floor, and saved himself only by clinging to Viv Martella's shoulder. She giggled. 'Whoops, sarge!'

It was a madhouse. If ever there was a morning when he ought to have found an excuse for staying in bed, this was it.

The gloom in the office was relieved only by a torch propped near the switchboard. Out of the semi-darkness swam the darker face of PC Lyttleton. It offered an opportunity to escape for a few minutes.

'Haven't shown you the outside facilities yet, have I, lad? Or the guest suite. Come and make yourself familiar with the layout.'

They went out into the yard, into the garage, and back along the narrow corridor between the cells. Cryer spun it out. He was in no hurry to plunge back into the general upheaval. Let Sergeant Tom Penny have a dose of it for a while.

Again he was seeing the nick from a different viewpoint. Not that there were many surprises left after all these years, least of all along here. Even the characters locked away behind those doors were getting repetitive. You'd have sworn that the same half-dozen types kept coming back month after month, year after year, without ever getting any older or any wiser.

He tugged back a shutter and peered in.

'Look at that. We do get some charmers, don't we?'

Drunk last night, the occupant of the cell was presumably

now sober, but looked little the better for it. Rhythmically he scratched his head like a monkey in a cage. When he saw Cryer looking in, he spat on the floor.

'So I see.' Lyttleton was still respectful and attentive.

In the background a shouting match began to build up. There were sounds of somebody thudding into a wall, kicking against a door. The noise grew louder. There was every indication that Sun Hill was on the verge of receiving another guest.

'Oh, come on, Ted,' Dashwood was panting. 'Give us a hand. Give us a . . .' He gasped, as if a fist or elbow had been skilfully planted in an uncomfortable spot.

Now Roach and Dashwood had manhandled their captive into the corridor, urging him towards a cell door. He was obviously reluctant to accept their hospitality. A squat man whose black singlet revealed broad shoulders and muscular arms, he was evidently well practised in using both. From his wide grimace and the enthusiasm of his kicking and punching, you might almost have thought that he enjoyed the whole process of being arrested and lashing out until the last possible minute.

'Get off me.' He managed a mighty heave which slammed Dashwood's shoulder against the wall.

'Come on, Plummer, come on.' Roach, too, appeared to be working off some accumulation of savage energy.

Cryer stepped forward and obligingly opened the cell door. Having done so, he stepped much more smartly back to avoid anything Plummer might try on his way in.

'I hope you catch AIDS, you slags.'

'Having to handle you,' Dashwood puffed, 'I wouldn't be at all . . . here, go on, *in* you go.'

There was a final heave, the thud of the door. Roach mopped his brow.

'Bastards,' came a yell from within.

Cryer grinned. 'Pleased to see you, was he?'

'I used me charm on him,' said Roach.

'Lousy perverts!'

'Be a copper and see the world, they told me.'

'You stink, the lot of yer.' When no reply was forthcoming, Plummer let out another roar. 'Sodding tossers. I wanna see Galloway.'

'All in good time,' said Roach.

They all moved away to put a muffling distance between themselves and the solo recitation of abuse echoing round the cell, and made their way through the front office. It was an unwise thing to do, as Bob Cryer realized the moment he set foot in it. One of the workmen began earnestly to explain that they had set up a temporary line but it couldn't cover all the equipment and mustn't be overloaded. Sergeant Penny was getting suddenly puritanical, complaining that the place was like a pigsty and trying to stack papers neatly at one end of a shelf while a man with a drill was showering crumbs of plaster on the other. And Jimmy Carver, who had gone out only twenty minutes earlier, was coming back in off the street with that pale, earnest look of his which meant that he was on to something and would not let go until someone had eased the pressure on him.

'Sarge, I tried to call in but nothing here seems to be answering.' He held out a slip of paper on which he had scribbled a registration number. 'Any chance of getting comms to run a vehicle check on this?'

'I think that some time in the next fortnight we might manage that,' said Cryer weightily. 'Always assuming the resumption of normal services. Reason?'

'Well, it's a Ford transit open-backed, and the tax disc number doesn't correspond with the vehicle.'

'Whereabouts?'

'Outside a boarded-up shop front on Queen's Parade. You know the place – been plated up with metal sheeting and planks for a couple of months now. Don't know what they're up to in there, but Taffy and me reckon it'll most likely be another Indian takeaway.'

'I'll have it checked out and let you know.'

'Thanks, sarge.'

'Off you go before you get electrocuted.'

Looking round, Cryer found that Ted Roach had deserted him. Perhaps he had gone in search of a cup of tea, since at this time of day there was nothing stronger available. He debated whether or not to go in search of him and ask just what Roy Galloway was up to, tearing in and out, issuing instructions for wheeling suspects in and then neglecting to state what they were suspected of. Then he remembered the state Roach was in, all because of the state Galloway was in; and decided to leave well alone until there was some sign of calm being restored.

All the same, he did wonder exactly what Galloway was after. Up to his usual game of trying to score off the uniformed branch, not letting on until he had satisfied his vanity with a single-handed victory?

What was it going to be *this* time?

Two

The path below the railway embankment had once led to a local station. Years ago the branch line had been cut off to make way for high-rise blocks of flats and a road junction, but nobody had got round to demolishing the abandoned station. Buildings and platform had been left to decay of their own accord. It was something they showed quite a talent for. On one side of the district, brash new buildings were going up. On the other, old ones were being left to rot. The world in between often appeared to have no idea of its own true identity; but at least its confusions and conflicts were on a scale to keep the local police in full employment.

Plodding along the path, whose verges were now a mess of encroaching weed, Detective Inspector Roy Galloway began the ascent of a seamed, cracked slope which had once been the main pedestrian approach to the station. He reached what was left of the platform. Ugly holes gaped before his feet. A waiting-room window was only a yawning gap. Any ghost using that room must have had a long wait by now.

He scuffed his shoes along the platform. There was no voice, no sound of any other movement in response.

'If I'm in the wrong place, Conga,' he said, loudly enough to carry above the rattle of a train along the embankment which now curved fastidiously away from the overgrown branch, 'I'm gonna kick your arse. But then if I am, you won't be hearing me anyway, so it'll come as a nice surprise when I *do* find you.'

'Got a way with words, you have, Mr Galloway. How's your luck, then?'

'Plenty of it. All bad.' Galloway edged closer to a wide gap in the end of the main building, taking care not to brush his jacket sleeve against the encrusted brickwork. The smell hit him. 'This is a piss-hole.'

It was all too true. The space beyond had once been the station gents'. This was something else which had not been pulled down; and he doubted if it had ever been washed down before the place was abandoned.

'Nice and quiet, though,' said Conga. 'Step into the office?'

Galloway stayed where he was. 'You got something for me, or what?'

'Get the pound notes out, Mr Galloway. It's a right good 'un.'

'Let's hear it, then.'

Another train racketed past. A face appeared between two rotting props, like safety bars in a nursery window. Conga's loose yellow jacket was slimed with shadow or with something else: he had not bothered to keep himself at a distance from the smeared walls. That was the story of Conga's life. He was used to getting contaminated, and had ceased to notice the taste and smell of it.

'A tunnel job,' he said hoarsely, pouting his lips at Galloway. 'A bank. On your patch. Interested?'

Galloway tingled. It was like coming out in prickly heat all down your back. It had always been like this with him, ever since he had started to climb his way up through the Force. Once you got a tingle of the right thing it began to burn you up. Conga stank, but Conga liked money, and Conga knew a lot about other stinking folk and would sell that knowledge for what he could get. It made Galloway sick and exultant at one and the same time.

He kept his voice sour and noncommittal. 'Depends.'

'Aw, come on.'

'Don't feed me a load of crap, my old son, or you and I could fall out. Understand?'

'Oh, I understand, Mr Galloway.' Conga was half sneering, half wheedling. 'You know me by now. I wouldn't do that.'

'You'd do anything.'

'That's not nice. Not nice at all.'

'Are you coming across' – Galloway found no difficulty in

letting the hard edge cut through his tone – 'or am I gonna have to do you for wasting my time?'

'All right. Two names, then. Frank Parry and Denny Lamb.'

'Where and when?'

'And the rest.' Conga could display his own bit of bravado. 'What about the rent? It's gotta be a good payer, a bank job.'

'You slimy git. What's the use of two names? Might as well expect a hand-out for telling me Marks & Spencer.'

'Oh, it's not Marks & Spencer, Mr Galloway. Like I told you, a bank. And like I told you, on your patch.'

'Come on, a lot more.'

They had played their ritual little duel, and now Conga told a lot more. It sounded plausible. It sounded better than plausible – or worse, as far as the bank was concerned, if it went ahead. Galloway knew the branch well enough and could see the logic of what Conga was telling him. Along Queen's Parade, right beside one of those derelict shops . . . oh, yes, that made good enough sense. And over this coming weekend? That made sense, too.

But he said: 'And why are you co-operating so nobly with the law this time, Conga?'

'Worth it, isn't it? You promised – '

'I haven't promised a single bloody note.'

'We've done useful business before, Mr Galloway. You wouldn't cheat on me this time, not when – '

'And just why are you cheating on your pals Parry and Lamb?'

'No pals of mine,' said Conga with sudden venom.

'Mm. This weekend?' said Galloway thoughtfully.

'That's the way I heard it.'

'This had better be kosher.'

'You'll see, Mr Galloway. And now, about the money – '

'Afterwards. When we've got 'em bang to rights.'

It was only as he walked away, quickening his pace down the path and across the road towards his car, that he wondered about Conga's readiness to trust him over the money. Usually they all wanted an immediate hand-out, and a big one. But maybe that was the difference between himself and Conga:

Conga knew him and trusted him; while he himself knew the likes of Conga and trusted none of them. Results were all that counted, on either side. This time he had a hunch he was going to get a result.

On the way back to Sun Hill he took a route including Queen's Parade. At least Conga hadn't fed him a dud when it came to the scenery. There it was, sure enough – the bank, and right beside it a shop which was not so much shuttered as armour-plated against vandals, with one metal door in its grey façade. Nice cosy neighbours. Only this time there wasn't going to be a neighbourly chat over the garden fence but a lot of quiet activity under the floor.

Galloway stopped on a double yellow line on the far side of the street. He fished in the glove compartment for his camera, waited for a dawdling bus to gather speed and get out of the way, and then took a series of shots: the frontage of the bank, the half-obscured sheeting of the shop front, the estate agent's sign angled out from the first floor, and the Ford truck piled with rubble and splintered timbers which was doing the obscuring.

Dropping the film in at DHQ for processing, he went back to the nick. Cryer's head turned inquiringly like that of a hopeful vulture as he went through, but Galloway continued nonstop up the stairs and was reaching for the phone before he sat down.

The bank manager sounded wary. 'The police?'

'Yes, sir. Detective Inspector Galloway from Sun Hill police station. Firstly, could you look in your file and find this station's number and call me straight back, please?'

'I'm not sure I understand, inspector. Are the police running out of coins for call boxes now, or have you mislaid your own number?'

Galloway kept his voice tightly courteous. 'I could give you my number, sir, but I want you to be sure of my identity.'

'This is something serious?'

'It is, sir.'

As Galloway put the receiver down he was in a better

humour than he had been all morning. He even managed an affable nod as Ted Roach came in.

'Right, Ted. Who's ready for a bit of excitement?'

'I think our Mr Plummer was enough excitement for one day, guv.'

'Come on, I warned you he likes a bit of a punch-up. You're getting a bit old, aren't you?'

'He's down in the cells. Not a happy chap.'

'My heart bleeds for him. Right,' Galloway went on briskly, 'forget about Plummer.'

'But guv, they want to know downstairs – '

'Something more urgent's come up.' He scribbled on his pad and tore off the sheet. 'I want you to get on to this firm of estate agents. Find out who's got the lease on the empty shop in Queen's Parade – around Number 20 or 22, I reckon it'll be – all right?'

'Right, guv. But what are we supposed to be looking for?'

'And then I want anything that Records can turn up on Frank Parry and Denny Lamb.' Before Roach could attempt any further questions the phone rang, and Galloway waved him away. 'Action. Right now.'

The door swung shut, but not before he had heard Roach snapping at Dashwood: 'How the hell does he expect us to work as a team when we don't know what the bloody hell's going on?'

The bank manager's voice was even more guarded than before. 'Detective Inspector . . . Galloway?'

'Thanks for getting back to me so quickly, sir. Now then . . .'

He got confirmation that the bank did indeed have those empty shop premises right next door. Yes, there was a party wall, with no intervening alley. No, the manager had not been aware of any unusual activity in the neighbouring basement. From the external appearance of the place and occasional movement outside he had assumed that new fitments were being installed, but could not say for what purpose: neither the previous tenant nor the agency handling the property were, he confided with some disdain, clients of his branch. He was a busy man. With so much to attend to in his own job, he had seen no reason to be concerned with what might be going on next door. Now, after a few questions and hints from Galloway, he began to feel very concerned; and very indignant.

When the conversation was over, Galloway beckoned to DC Dashwood through the glass partition.

'Get on to the Civil Engineer's Department at the Town Hall. I want a complete set of plans covering properties on Queen's Parade. Both sides of the road.'

'All right, guv.'

'And if they ask any questions, use your charm without giving anything away.'

'How can I give anything away, guv? I don't know what's going on.'

Galloway's fragile mood of elation began to cloud over. He did not like the smell of insubordination permeating the place. But as Dashwood went, Ted Roach came back and the demands of the job came back.

'Right, Ted, what've you got?'

There was not a lot. The property was up for let and had been on the market now for six months. The owner was a Mr Bryinski, but he was out of the country and had been so for some weeks. Nothing had been said about him leaving any instructions for builders, decorators, or anything like that, though the agents thought he could well have done so without necessarily notifying them.

'Listen, guv, with the greatest respect, where does Plummer come into all this?'

'Plummer?' Galloway stared blankly. 'Oh, him. He doesn't.'

'Then why the hell . . .'

Sergeant Cryer stood in the doorway, holding out a packet. 'Here we are, Roy. Just arrived by messenger from DHQ. Very urgent.'

'Great.' Galloway snatched the envelope of photographs from Cryer's hand.

'You been going round the back door again?'

'Ted, I want you, Chris and Jim ready for a briefing the

minute Mike gets back. And call your wives and lovers, you're liable to be on overtime.'

'Cheers.' Roach shoved resentfully past Bob Cryer.

When he had gone, Cryer said: 'Anything we should know, Roy?'

'Thanks for the delivery, Robert.'

'Oh. So the Lone Ranger's alive and well and living in Sun Hill nick, is he?'

'You'll be informed, if and when.'

'Wonderful. By the way, what are you going to do about your Mr Plummer? We can't hold him much longer without a charge, you know.'

Galloway was impatiently slitting open the envelope, wanting to be alone with the contents. 'Well, he assaulted Detective Sergeant Roach, didn't he? Charge him with that for now.'

The briefing began the moment Mike Dashwood had pinned the photographs and the map to a pegboard, propped against the partition like a shield against prying eyes.

'We're assuming they're going to come in from the shop basement. Doesn't make sense any other way.' Galloway tapped the dark line between the bank and its neighbour. 'Once they're through this flank wall here, it's only a matter of digging through about twelve and a half feet of clay and they're directly below the vault floor. It's that simple. Any questions?'

'Do we know how they intend getting up through the vault floor?'

'I've received no direct information on that score,' said Galloway heavily. 'Making an educated guess, I'd say they'll attempt a series of small charges. Parry and Lamb seem to have a record of only petty stuff so far, but Frank Parry has form with explosives. Looks like he's ready to branch out.'

'Into the branch, you might say,' beamed Jim Ellis.

'I might, but I wouldn't.'

'When do we go in?' asked Roach.

This was the tricky one. Galloway had been mulling it over in his mind. Every instinct urged him to strike now and make a killing. But common sense advised otherwise. 'If we dive in too early our friends might duck any real charges. I think we've got to let them dig away until they're right under the money. It's ten to one they won't go for it until the weekend. Bank break-ins are nearly always weekend stuff.'

'The bank's been informed, guv?'

'It has. I'm having another meeting with the manager once we've drawn up our programme. But I'm not aiming to have every tinpot clerk there gawping out of the windows and playing Sherlock Holmes.'

'Do the uniform lads know the score yet?'

'No, they do not,' said Galloway fiercely. 'I'm not aiming to have a crowd of bloody woodentops trampling all over everything, either, and frightening our little firm away. For the moment I want this treated strictly as an obbo number. Observe, that's all. Everything has to stay the way it is, nice and normal, until I say otherwise.'

'Firearms, guv?' suggested Ellis.

'Not Parry and Lamb. Not from their record. That'd be way out of their line. Okay, that's it. Jim, clear this away and shift those pictures. Ted and Mike, take first turn as of now. Get down below, Mike. Ted, come and have a look at this.' Galloway took down the plan and spread it on the desk, indicating a side street at an angle from the bank. 'From what I've seen of the site I think the best place for you is here. And if Mike sits over *there*, you'll both have good views of the shop front. All right?'

Roach nodded dubiously. 'But we won't have a visual on each other.' He leaned over the map, probing. 'Now, if I sat here – '

'No, Ted. Look – '

'And Mike sits here. Much better.'

'Do it my way, all right?'

'With due respect, sir – '

'Look,' Galloway exploded, 'I haven't got time for a debate. Christ, what's up with you lately?'

'What's up with *me*? That's bloody marvellous, coming from

you. Bloody marvellous, that is.'

'Now come on, what's all this about?'

'You really want me to tell you, inspector?'

'Oh, don't push it, Ted.'

'*Do* you want me to tell you? Really?'

They glared at each other until Roach turned abruptly and quit the room.

In the morning June Ackland was almost sent flying as DI Galloway went through the front office without uttering a good morning to Bob Cryer or even nodding when Tom Penny held the door at the foot of the stairs open for him. The two sergeants nodded at each other and shrugged. Lonely nights and an empty bed: none of it made for happy days.

Cryer looked cheerful enough, anyway. The VDU was working, the new switchboard was in good order, the lights were on. It was business as usual.

Including the inevitable first bit of trouble, as usual.

Taffy Edwards, at the switchboard, looked back over his shoulder. 'Woodclose Primary – that's not on your patch, is it, Yorkie?'

'Not for a couple of months now. I did go up there that once to do the "love your local bobby and don't talk to strangers" act. Do they want an encore?'

'It's the headmaster, Mr Davis. Says there's a kid gone missing. They're worried about her.'

'Gone missing?' said June Ackland. 'At this time of the morning? I wouldn't have thought they'd even have finished prayers yet.'

'If you run along quickly,' said Cryer, 'you might be in time for some spiritual uplift.'

'You mean you want *me* to go, sarge?'

'That was the general drift of it, yes.'

June sighed and reached for her cap.

It was a mild but gusty morning. Sunlight on the far pavement of Sun Hill suggested there might once have been some justification for its name before the warehouse, factory and police station walls rose to cast their long shadows. The brightness failed, though, to penetrate the playground of Woodclose Primary, a barracks of heavy brick in the same dour style as its neighbouring apartment blocks. All the school windows were barred on the outside, and as the headmaster led June up a flight of cracked steps he helped to haul himself up by clutching green-painted iron struts in the stair arches.

On the landing he stopped, his podgy chest heaving, and explained. Samantha Welsh was eight years old, very shy and not a girl for making melodramatic gestures. Plenty of Woodclose pupils played truant from time to time, and Mr Davis would not have been too distressed if some of them failed to show up ever again. But Samantha was not that type. She was an obedient child, with a very proper and watchful mother. When Samantha failed to show up this morning he had rung her home, and Mrs Welsh came round immediately.

'And the father?'

Davis paused with his hand on the knob of his study door. 'I don't know him so well. He doesn't come to the school very often, not even for parents' evenings. He's West Indian, a bus driver.'

'Any other children?'

'No.'

Davis opened the door. Mrs Welsh, sitting on the edge of a chair and twisting her fingers over the strap of her handbag, half got up, looked from one face to the other, and then untwisted the fingers of her right hand and dabbed helplessly at a loose strand of hair.

'Now, Mrs Welsh.' Davis spoke with well-meaning but rather unctuous benevolence. 'Don't be alarmed. I'm sure that with this young lady's help we can all . . . er . . . sort something out. Now, Miss . . . er . . .'

'Ackland. WPC Ackland.'

'Thank you, Miss . . . PC Ackland . . . Mrs Welsh.'

The woman stared challengingly at June, as if to say that anyone in that uniform, with hair that clean and crisp, ought to be just as crisp and official in settling everything on the spot.

June tried to sound direct and confident.'Samantha left home this morning at the usual time?'

'Oh, I've already told Mr Davis that. Of course she did. I always make sure she's got everything ready the moment she gets up, so she doesn't cut things too fine. Always the same time, to the minute.'

'She enjoys coming to school?'

'Of course she does.'

'I can vouch for that,' said the headmaster. 'She's a quiet girl, but very conscientious.'

'She hasn't said anything about bullying, or anything of that sort?'

Mrs Welsh shook her head.

June took a deep breath. 'I'm sorry to have to ask you this, but has there been anything at home recently that could have upset her?'

Mrs Welsh bristled. 'Whatever do you mean?'

'Well, just if someone's been cross with her. Or if there's been any kind of trouble between you and your husband. If, as Mr Davis says, she's a quiet, sensitive sort of girl – '

'No.'

The answer was so sharp that June wanted to frame some more roundabout way of asking the same question so that she could get a more helpful line on things. But Mrs Welsh was getting up from the chair.

'I really ought to be getting back. I phoned the bus station for my husband to come home as soon as he could. He was going to have a look round on his way back. He might have had some luck. He . . . or Sammy might have come back while I've been here.'

It would be nice all round to have it tidied up that simply. June felt a chill of doubt in the air. All three of them were nodding now and trying to look cheerful and shrug it off and assure each other that this was how it was going to happen.

'Look, I'll pop in and see you later on,' she said. 'You know, pick up a photograph.'

That spoiled the atmosphere of optimism right away.

'Yes,' said Mrs Welsh hoarsely.

When the mother had gone, June looked glumly at the headmaster. Something was not quite right. On impulse she said, 'Is the kid really as . . . well, shy . . . conscientious, you said?'

'I wouldn't want to worry the mother unnecessarily until we have our end-of-term reports and parents' meeting.'

'So there's something else? Something to worry about?'

Reluctantly Davis opened the second drawer of his desk and sorted through a sheaf of papers. He offered one to June. 'Samantha has tended to be a bit slapdash in her written work this term,' he admitted. 'She ought to spend less time dreaming.'

'Hm. Any reason for the dreaming?'

'Nothing at all evident. Children do go through phases, you know, and we try not to jump to any cut-and-dried conclusions.'

June skimmed down the entries on the interim report. 'I see it says here that she has been having some problems with – what's this? – relationships within the group.'

Davis leaned over her. 'Ah, yes. Miss Horrocks. Probably means that Samantha doesn't talk enough in class. When she's spoken to, that is.' He attempted a watery smile.

'Does she seem lonely?'

The headmaster fidgeted. He was forever flicking an imaginary speck from his cardigan, rubbing his lower lip, or glancing from side to side in an appeal for help that refused to come.

'Well,' he said, 'she *has* struck up a friendship this term, so I suppose that ought to make her less lonely than before. A girl called Theresa O'Brien. Odd mixture, really. Irish family – one of eight.'

'Can I see her?'

'Naturally.' The headmaster looked momentarily smug. 'I've already arranged for her to come along. But I thought it best to have Mrs Welsh off the premises first.' As if on cue, there was a tap at the door. 'Come in.'

A thin woman with straw-coloured hair and aggrieved, straw-coloured eyes opened the door and ushered in a girl whose dark hair and deep-set eyes appeared all the darker in contrast.

'Thank you, Miss Horrocks.'

June would have liked a few minutes longer to assess the teacher who was apparently dissatisfied with Samantha's speechlessness in class; but Miss Horrocks fussed out and was gone.

'Right.' Davis pulled a chair forward. 'Come and sit down, Theresa.' His hand on her shoulder forced her gently on to the chair. 'Nothing to be frightened of. The police lady wants to ask you one or two questions, that's all.'

'I ain't done nothing.'

'We didn't think you had,' said June. 'I just want you to tell me a bit about Samantha. Now, Mr Davis says you're friends.'

The girl stared, mute.

'You walk to school together?'

Theresa shook her head. Her thumb found its way to the corner of her mouth.

'Go home together sometimes, then?'

At last there was a response. 'Part of the way.'

'And when you're on your way home, do you ever go off anywhere for a while?' Now it was a head shake again. 'Don't you nip into a playground, a park, anywhere like that? Do you have somewhere secret, just the two of you?' Another lowering, silent denial. 'Theresa . . . when you've been with Samantha, has anyone ever come up and talked to you? Offered you sweets, anything like that?'

The child kept solemnly shaking her head. The steadfast denial seemed genuine enough, yet there was an odd, calculating gleam in her eyes. When the headmaster had sent her back to her classroom he asked apprehensively:

'You think there's a possibility Samantha might have gone off with somebody?'

'We have to consider it, that's all. It's one in a million. Look, it's just that if you should hear of anyone hanging about – '

'Yes, yes, of course.' He cut her short, not wanting to hear. 'Yes, you may be sure.'

June drove round to the address she had been given on the Riverdale estate. The Elizabeth Garrett Anderson block was like a score of other blocks in this part of the world, where modernization had meant devastation. Somewhere a baby was crying forlornly. From an open window came the competition of a radio babbling out pop song titles in mounting hysteria. She picked her way over a morass of torn newspapers and crushed drink cans, and went up to the third landing in a lift scrawled over with obscenities.

She had hardly taken her thumb off the bell push when the door was flung open. The expectant look in Mrs Welsh's eyes faded, telling her that Samantha was not yet back.

'I've come to pick up the photograph.'

They went inside. June sat on a sofa with a pattern in mauve curlicues as Mrs Welsh leafed through an album, watched over by a large framed colour print on the sideboard. In all the pictures Samantha's creamy, coffee-coloured face with its deeper brown eyes looked demure, composed, but unsmiling.

June selected a head-and-shoulders picture, and a full-length one. Mrs Welsh watched them go from their usual place with a slight shiver, and reached for a cigarette.

'You've got a phone so you can call us if she turns up?'

'Not in here, no.'

'But you said something about ringing your husband.'

'From the box downstairs. On the ground floor, near the lift.'

'Well, I'll be back at the station if you've got anything to report. Any good news,' said June encouragingly. 'And we'll send out a call, see what we can do. Mr Welsh'll be back soon?'

Mrs Welsh shrugged. She was beginning to look as if she did not believe in anybody ever coming back.

June reported in, and the message went out to all units. Girl, half West Indian, missing, eight years old, hair tied back, wearing a pale blue anorak, green tartan skirt and white socks. answering to the name of Samantha Welsh. Last seen at her home . . .

It was less than an hour later when Mr Davis showed up at the desk with Theresa in tow. June Ackland was on her way to the canteen, but swung round as she saw Sergeant Penny leaning over the counter and beginning to ask questions.

'Mr Davis' – she hurried towards him ' – anything to report?'

'Oh, it's you. Good. It was you I wanted to see. Most urgently. Felt I had to come round, have a quiet word.'

'Sarge, is anyone using the interview room?'

Penny waved her towards the door along the corridor. Theresa, head down, let herself be shepherded through by the headmaster.

'Take a seat.' June offered Theresa a friendly smile. The girl looked down at her toes. 'Right, what seems to be the latest?'

'I'm afraid Theresa didn't tell you everything,' said Davis. 'She thought it might be a sin.'

Three

Galloway sat staring at the folded sheet of paper on his desk, willing himself not to open it and re-read it for the tenth time this morning. It was cold, clear and impersonal and it had come as no surprise; yet still, though he had been waiting for it, he did not want to believe it. One more glance, ten more glances, would only make it more and more believable.

He tried to drag his mind away and concentrate on the important issues of the moment. Roach and Dashwood had reported in on their observation during the night. None of it added up to anything exciting. The two targets had spent all evening in the Monk's Head pub, leaving only at closing time. Lamb had then dropped Parry off at his place around 11.45 and had got back to his own pad just after midnight. Both of them home to bed like good little boys: evidently they were not yet doing late-night shifts under the bank. Maybe that was being saved up for the weekend.

Galloway wanted action right now, but knew his decision yesterday just had to be the right one. Moving too soon would spoil everything.

His hand went out to that paper again. Then, as if acting entirely without his authority, it lifted the phone. He dialled the familiar number.

Something was sticking and aching in his stomach. He waited for Maureen to answer, as she had answered hundreds of times when he rang from this very office, this very phone – usually to tell her that he had got caught up in an urgent job and would be late home.

It was not Maureen who answered, but Julia.

The pain grew worse. Somehow it twisted itself over on itself, wrenching at him, before he could speak. 'Julia, it's me. It's dad.'

There was silence save for a faint singing note along the line, then: 'What do you want?'

'Well, just to say hello. You know. How are you?'

'Mum,' she was calling, 'it's dad on the phone.'

Maureen was the one he had been meaning to speak to, but now he wanted to postpone it. 'Julia, don't call your mum yet.'

Too late. 'Hello?' said Maureen, cold and very far away.

'Sorry to call you at this hour of the morning.'

'What do you want, Roy?'

'I . . . I just got the divorce papers through. I just thought we ought to talk.'

'Talk? You want to *talk*?' He could almost hear her silently reciting the catalogue of his iniquities, the late nights, the days when he had been too busy to get home for more than half an hour at a time, or too exhausted to be any kind of company.

He tried: 'Look, please – '

'You've left it just a little bit too late. About ten years too bloody late.'

She had smacked the receiver down. He clawed at the paper yet again, knowing nothing could wipe out those legal, formal words. He threw it across the office just as Bob Cryer came in.

'Sorry, Roy.' One look at his face, and Cryer was already turning away. 'I'll come back.'

'What is it?'

'Well, your Mr Plummer. We've got him banged up still. Been here all night, remember? Kept asking for you at breakfast time.'

'Did he, now?'

'Taffy Edwards asked whether he wanted you grilled or fried.'

'That must have gone down well.'

'He chucked the breakfast all over Taffy.'

Galloway could not even raise a smile. 'All right, I'll be down.'

'Cell or truth room?'

'What?'

'Do you want to interview him in the cell,' said Cryer patiently, 'or in an interview room?'

'Leave him to stew in the cell.'

'Fine.' Cryer paused in the doorway. 'You all right, mate?'

'Fine. Why shouldn't I be?'

Galloway gave himself a couple of minutes to stop his stomach heaving, then went down to confront Plummer.

'And about bloody well time, too.' Plummer swung his legs off the bunk and crouched forward as if ready to butt the DI in the stomach. 'Just what am I supposed to be here for?'

Cryer listened with some interest. The answer to this question was one for which he, too, had been kept waiting.

'You know what,' said Galloway. 'Roach must have told you in the vehicle.'

'Didn't tell me nothing. Ignorant git.'

'Armed robbery on the night of the eighteenth of April. How does that grab you?'

'Come off it. You must be joking.'

Galloway was in no joking mood. Neither was he any longer really interested. The whole business of Plummer had been a bit of a flyer, and he had known it all along. Right now he was a lot more concerned about what might be going on under Queen's Parade. But he was not prepared to let this greasy little villain get away scot-free.

'According to information received – '

'Stuff that. For *your* information, on the night of the eighteenth of April – and on the seventeenth and the twenty-first, come to think of it – I was spending some interesting hours with a lady of my acquaintance.'

'If you can't do better than that, you're in dead lumber.'

'You got me shivering in me boots, chief.' Plummer's evil little sneer goaded Galloway on.

'Who was she, this old slag you're supposed to have been knocking off?'

'Never mentioned old slag. No way. A lady, I said.'

'So on the night in question you were shacked up with a

mystery. Okay. Who was she, what's her name?'

'Now come on, chief. Can't tell you that, now, can I? A married woman, see. Wouldn't be right if I told, know what I mean?'

Galloway snorted. 'And what would rubbish like you know about what's right, eh?'

'Be fair, chief, you know how it is. I mean' – Plummer leaned insinuatingly closer – 'it might well have been your own old woman I was humping.'

All the pain and rage came up from Galloway's heart and stomach. From his very guts. He hurled himself forward, dragged Plummer up to his feet and hurled him against the far wall of the cell.

'Leave it, Roy!'

Cryer was trying to get between them. Galloway elbowed him aside and began to smash his fist into Plummer's face, smashing that filthy bloody head back against the wall, again and again.

'Leave it. Enough, Roy!'

Cryer got his arm round Galloway's throat and dragged him away. They swayed together, panting.

Plummer was wiping his bloodied mouth. 'He's a nutter. A flaming nutter.'

'You shut it,' snarled Cryer.

'Bleeding nut. I'll have him nicked for that.'

'I said shut it.' Cryer hammered on the door to be let out. Galloway lurched out ahead of him and leaned against the cold wall of the corridor, waiting for the place to stop going red and blue and all the colours of the rainbow. He tried to make his heartbeat slow down. He still wanted – it was all he wanted – to kill that stinking scum in there. He hardly heard what Cryer was growling at him. 'That was brilliant, Roy. That was really brilliant.'

He found words. 'Get rid of him.'

'What, Plummer? But you – '

'Chuck him out. While he's still alive.'

★

June Ackland tried it again, slowly and carefully. This was something you did not dare to get wrong.

'And you were with Samantha when you saw this man? But you didn't tell anybody about it – not even your mum?'

'No,' whispered Theresa.

'Can you tell me what the man looked like?' As the girl's head sank again and she looked sideways with that odd, sly expression of hers, June said more forcefully: 'Come on, my love. Samantha's your friend, isn't she? Hm?'

Theresa nodded.

'Well, I want you to think very hard, because we want to try and find her, don't we?'

Theresa considered this for what seemed an age. Even her eventual nod seemed equivocal. June was suddenly scared that the kid would freeze up – reluctant to come out with the full story in the first place, she had now said all she dared to say and was wishing she had kept quiet about it after all.

'How old was this man?' June probed. 'Some young feller, was it?'

'Oh, no.'

'How old, then?'

'Well, you know ... quite old.'

'Older than ... well, Mr Davis?'

'No.'

'Now, did he say anything to you when you saw him?'

Theresa was shaking her head again.

'What, then?'

'Well, like I told you.' The girl seemed to be thinking of something else, somewhere to the left of her left shoe. 'His mac, and all that.'

'He was wearing a mac? Not an overcoat, or a windcheater?'

'No.'

It was hard going. The whole wretched business was taking on a new dimension. Missing persons, missing kids, were one part of the job. There were dozens of reasons why people wandered off, and then got bored or frightened and wandered back again. Once it ceased to be a 'misper' and became a matter of real danger, of flashers and possible abductors, then it was a different game. And everybody at Sun Hill had to be in on it.

Galloway called in his obbo forces from Queen's Parade. The message to patrol units was repeated, but with a more sinister emphasis. Bob Cryer set up an emergency briefing in the parade room. Usually there were jokes, moans and groans. Before the meeting started, Taffy Edwards was grumbling about not getting away in time to catch a train to North Wales and the girl who would be waiting for him at the station, and Reg Hollis was complaining that his back trouble had got so much worse that he simply couldn't be expected to stand and listen to a procedural lecture for more than five minutes at most. Well within the five minutes they were all grimly silent and attentive. A runaway kid might have provoked snide remarks about parents and bloody schools and half-witted schoolmasters. Changed circumstances made for changed attitudes.

Galloway had taken charge. 'This misper is going to be treated as an abduction from now on. Which means that whatever's going on we have to get at it fast, and stop it. Bob, I'd like you and Martella to do house-to-house right through the flats. You both know that territory better than anyone. The rest of you . . .'

He assembled the programme with all his old, bitter commitment. If it had been his own daughter, his Julia, at that age – well no, he wasn't going to think of that; but it cleared his mind to think about somebody else, some other little girl who was still an abstract figure to all of them here but who was going to be saved and protected if he had anything to do with it. Lyttleton and Carver were assigned to the timber yard on the edge of Riverdale. And when they had finished turning that over, they could start along the dock road and look at every crumbling wharf, every little inlet. Hollis and Muswell were detailed to search the grounds and sheds, basements, boiler-rooms, rubbish dumps, anything whatever around the blocks of flats. Hollis flinched at the prospect. 'Look, sir, I'm still having treatment for my back, you know. If I have to do any heavy lifting, moving things aside, sort of . . .' Galloway ignored him. 'Ackland, you'll be liaison with the parents. Find out if their kid mentioned anything about this flasher.'

'Don't you think Mrs Welsh would have told me already?'

'Maybe, maybe not. Either way it's time to make sure they know the whole picture.'

Bob Cryer said: 'Look, Roy, you don't often get a flasher going in for abduction. It's two separate types. Flashers usually scuttle for cover the moment they've given themselves an airing. Of all the cases we've had on this manor – '

'I know, Bob. But Theresa whatsername has reported a flasher, and Samantha Welsh was there with her, and now Samantha's gone missing. Maybe this time we've got a nasty mixture – two different things both coming to the boil at once. So let's move, right?'

They moved. A dog-handler showed up in his van just as Lyttleton and Carver were piling into a panda car. Bob Cryer and Viv Martella began their wearying, watchful plod round the flats, up and down in the lifts, along every landing. Ted Roach and Mike Dashwood began riffling through lists of known sex offenders on the manor and beyond it, indulging in a few sour reminiscences and discarding one impossibility after another. Even some of the possibilities seemed improbable. There was still no helpful pattern. The trouble with this sort of exercise was that patterns took time to establish themselves, and by the time you'd got round to recognizing them it could be too late. Round up the culprit, fine; but not so fine for the injured, terrified kid who had had to suffer while you were working out the permutations.

June Ackland went back to the door which Mrs Welsh had hopefully and then despondently opened for her once before. Even before she reached it she could hear the yelling from within.

'Oh, it's always my bleeding fault, isn't it?' This was no longer the respectable Mrs Welsh so approvingly spoken of by the headmaster. 'I wish you'd go and do yourself a – '

'Shut up.'

'I just wish you were – '

'All right, what? You go right ahead, woman, you tell me what.'

June pressed the bell. There was an immediate hush, as if a radio had been abruptly switched off. Mrs Welsh opened the door. 'Oh.' She looked taken aback, then eager again. 'Any news?'

'No. It's just really to keep you in the picture.' When there was no reaction, June added casually: 'May I come in?'

'Oh. Oh, yes, sorry.'

'Is Mr Welsh back yet?' It hardly needed answering, but it was a tactful pretence.

'He's in the lounge.' Mrs Welsh prodded a stiff right arm towards the inner door. 'Please go through.'

Welsh was standing at the window, surveying the world below. He was slim and good-looking, almost graceful in his weariness. It was the weariness – an innate, sad sort of smothered resignation – which struck June at first sight. She had glimpsed it momentarily in PC Abe Lyttleton, the dark suspicion and the instinctive readiness to endure insults; but Abe had stuck his neck out and fought it by joining the police force – inviting all kinds of trouble rather than waiting for it to come at him.

'I see you have a search party.' Welsh did not even turn round to greet their visitor, but went on staring down. 'They're at the rubbish dump now.'

'Please don't,' whimpered Mrs Welsh. She was timid and shrunken again, now.

June Ackland kept her voice reassuring. 'It's normal procedure.'

'For you, maybe,' said Welsh.

It was difficult to know where to start; or, rather, where to pick up and start all over again. It was only by niggling away that there was a chance of something new being said, some fresh lead being given.

'Mr Welsh. Mrs Welsh. I'm sorry, but we do have to try . . . look, you're sure Samantha never mentioned any worries?

Anything that could have upset her? Mr Davis did suggest that her work had slipped a bit recently. Do you have any idea why?'

Welsh looked sullenly at his wife, who grew suddenly snappish. 'It's that Theresa, that's what. Look, I try to keep her away, but you can't. Not all the time, and not when they're in school anyhow.'

'You don't approve of Theresa?'

'She . . . puts her up to things. I can tell. *And* she even gave her the nits.'

'Her other school friends – does she ever go anywhere with them?'

'No.' Mrs Welsh was taut and self-righteous. 'She always comes straight home. I've always dinned that into her.'

June turned to Welsh, who had sat down for a moment but was unable to remain still. As she spoke he was already pushing up on to his feet again, drawn wretchedly to the window.

'Mr Welsh, what about places she might have been with you?'

His wife answered for him. 'She don't go to a lot of places, not really. Damon takes her out once in a while. On the buses, swimming baths, you know. Oh, and we went to that panto at Stratford last Christmas. We all three went.' For some reason she emphasized the last remark.

Brooding, Welsh left her to it. June tried to bring him into the conversation. 'Do you go anywhere particular on the buses?'

'Just usual places.'

'Such as?'

'Oh, the zoo.'

'Yes?' she prompted.

'Museums. Er . . . *Cutty Sark*.'

'That wasn't all that recent,' said his wife.

They were both quietly desperate yet could not bring themselves to dig down into the real facts and bring them out for display. June said: 'I know you're both naturally very anxious, and I don't want you to jump to conclusions. But we're having to consider every kind of possibility, however slight.'

Mrs Welsh was reaching for another cigarette. Ash already made a wispy trail down one side of her cardigan.

'Has Samantha ever mentioned a man to you?' June persevered.

She had at last got through to Welsh. 'What kind of man?'

'We've had a statement from . . . from one of the children that a man exposed himself to her and Samantha. Now, it could well be unconnected, but we're having to consider all the possibilities.'

'You keep saying that!'

She let it simmer for a moment, then said: 'Do you mind if I have a look in her room before I go?'

'Normal procedure?' said Welsh caustically.

'As a matter of fact, yes.'

For a moment she thought he was going to reach out and grab her, shake her, just to relieve his pent-up feelings. Then he jerked his head. 'The next room. Through there.'

It was the kind of room you would have expected to find: a kid's bedroom, with a few of her own blobby paintings pinned to a board, a scattering of toys, and a large brown rabbit on the bed, minus one ear.

'Benjamin Bunny,' said Welsh, tight-lipped.

'What happened to his ear? Mr Macgregor get him?'

He managed a smile. 'She chews it. Look, miss, I'm sorry if –'

'It's a lousy time for you.' She picked up a drawing on a crumpled sheet of white paper. 'The *Cutty Sark*?'

'No, that's meant to be St Katharine's Dock, last year. I promised to take her again, but . . .' He hunched his shoulders defensively. 'You know how it is. The things you don't get round to.'

On the bedside locker was another picture with a touch of the sea and a distant boat in the background. This time it was no scrawl, but a bright and cheerful photograph. In the foreground were Welsh and his daughter. He had his arm round her shoulders, apparently trying to lift her off her feet, and she was smiling at the camera – one of the few unaffectedly smiling studies of her June had so far seen.

Welsh followed the direction of her gaze. 'Margate, last summer.'

'Your wife took it?'

'No, a photographer on the front. My wife was in hospital. You know, women's things.'

'But she's okay now?'

'Yes,' he said dourly. 'Perfectly all right.'

There was nothing more to be done here. June left, promising to be in touch as soon as there was any news. It was hard to decide who looked the more disbelieving: Welsh or his wife.

Dashwood had come up with two names. They were both local, and both on the loose right now. Terence Lowe, thirty-seven years of age, had raped a twelve-year-old and been given a life sentence. But he was out now, had been out just a month.

'Some bloody shrink, I suppose,' said Dashwood, 'giving him the all-clear to start all over again.'

'We're just checking up on him, Mike,' Ted Roach warned. 'No jumping to conclusions.'

Then there was Derek Hammond. His record was one of rather pathetic interferences, most of them bungled: no violence, no rape, just flashing and touching up little girls and then running away – until the law caught up with him. A short sentence, and a recommended course of psychiatric treatment. For his own good, naturally . . . if it worked.

Two likely ones, then. Find them and eliminate them; or clobber them.

Roach and Dashwood set off on the trail.

Muswell and Hollis clambering over rubbish tips, June Ackland asking the parents the same questions yet again in the hope of detecting one significant alteration in their story, Carver and Lyttleton pacing along dockside and towpath while divers went down into the choked waters of a canal, Roach and Dashwood pursuing men whose names just happened to be linked with the sort of crime this might or might not be: they couldn't all be on the right track. Maybe none of them was. Maybe while they were sieving evidence and suspicions in a dozen distinct ways, the real truth was somewhere else and nobody yet had even the beginnings of a relevant lead. It was simply a matter of covering every possibility and faint theory, saturating the area and then analysing the results in the hope that somewhere in the mess there was one nugget of truth.

Terence Lowe was not at home. His neighbour, a blonde with long legs and a very short white skirt, was languidly stretching out a long bare arm to paint a windowframe as Roach and Dashwood arrived. She seemed pleased by the diversion, alternately reaching up from the stepladder and leaning out from it to present some interesting viewpoints to the visitors. Her physical assets stimulated the imagination; but her spoken words were unhelpful. She was unable to offer any information about Mr Lowe except that he had gone away and asked her to cancel the milk. No, she had no idea where he had gone or how long he would be. It was not, she said archly, that they were all that *close*. Just good neighbours, that was all.

Driving slowly away, Roach radioed a request for the collator to put out a bulletin for the whereabouts of Terence Lowe. Reluctantly he stole one last glance at the blonde in his mirror, narrowly missed an oncoming truck, and forced himself to drive steadily and soberly to their next port of call.

'If it's Hammond,' he observed, 'the kid's in luck.'

'Luck, you call it?'

'He wouldn't hurt a fly.'

'Oh, no, he just takes little girls and – '

'I said *hurt*. Anyway, he's been out nearly two years and we haven't had word of any trouble. I think I'd have heard.'

'Why you in particular?'

'I was the one who nicked him.'

They drew up outside a block of modern council flats, clean but uninspiring, opposite a terrace of older houses sagging into dereliction.

Hammond was also not at home. He was out at work, his mother explained proudly. They weren't going to cause him trouble, were they, now that he'd got a job? It wouldn't be fair, not after all he'd been through and all the hard work he was doing now. Roach made reassuring noises. Dashwood looked sceptical and wrinkled his nose as if some nasty smell had reached it from along the landing.

Next call was the garage where Hammond was working. A quarter of an hour later he was in the Sun Hill interview room. He had whined protests all the way here in the car, and he was still protesting.

'It's nothing to do with me. Just because I've got previous. I haven't touched a kid since I've been out. Honest. You got no right to try and nail me just because – '

'Listen, my friend,' said Roach. 'We are not trying to nail you. We're trying to eliminate you from our enquiries. For your sake as well as ours. Now, you left for work this morning at eight fifteen, right?'

'I always do.'

'And you got to work about nine fifteen. Wasn't that rather a long time?'

'Now listen – '

'No. *You* listen. With a thing like this, and with your record, people are bound to point the finger. Eh? Now, answer my questions and then you're free to go.'

'You're not going to keep me here?'

'I don't want to have to.'

Roach was sure in his bones that Hammond was not guilty. He had to go through the procedure, but however little faith Hammond might have in his assurances, he genuinely wanted to eliminate the poor little freak and get him off the premises. The truth was somewhere else. He was sure of it.

He felt a twinge of complacency when Galloway called him out with a piece of news relayed from the national computer. Terence Lowe not only had the London house but rented two small flats over drinking clubs he managed: one in Brighton, one in Margate. The name of Margate had rung a bell with June Ackland. The kid's father had taken her there once, and it seemed to have been a place where she was happy. It might not have taken much to coax her back there.

With a bit of luck Lowe would be picked up in Margate. Or in

Brighton – alone or otherwise. Maybe it could all be wrapped up neatly this very day. That was how DI Galloway certainly wanted it, so that he could put Roach and Dashwood back on full-time surveillance of that shop and bank before the weekend, before it was too late. That was how it seemed to be turning out.

Until Carver and Lyttleton, late in the afternoon, arrived with a witness and quite a different tale to tell, and quite different implications to be followed up.

They had drawn a blank in the timber yard and were crossing the road towards the channel between river and old dock when a Ford transit clattered past. Carver froze on the edge of the pavement as the vehicle careered round a boarded-up warehouse and was lost to view.

'I'd swear that was that dodgy numberplate job.'

'Not our job right this minute.'

'I'd still like to nab that one. When I get another look at Queen's Parade, if they're still – '

'Right this minute,' Abe Lyttleton insisted sombrely, 'we're looking for flesh and blood, not dodgy discs and plates.' As they fell into step he added: 'Got a couple of my own, round about that age.'

They paced along the water's edge, looking down but not wanting to find anything.

'Where were you born, then?' asked Jimmy Carver.

'The sunshine state of Hackney, my son.'

'Really. So what made you join the police force?'

'What's this, the first round of Mastermind?'

'Sorry.'

'It's all right.' Lyttleton slowed to study a tangle of weed trailing across the water, and dismissed it. 'I get asked that all the time. I joined because' – he ventured a self-deprecatory grin – 'I wanted to do something worthwhile. And you?'

Carver answered him grin for grin. 'More or less the same reason.'

They made their way down to the wide basin, derelict a few

years ago but now beginning to glow with refurbished sheds and a number of brightly painted barges.

'Her father brought her to St Katharine's Dock last year,' said Carver. 'Could have walked her anywhere along here, or up that bank.'

'Talk about clutching at straws.' Lyttleton stared unhappily into the water. It was getting a hypnotic hold on him. 'They'll be sending the diving team down here too, any time now.'

The two of them stopped beside a gangplank. At its far end an elderly man with a matted yellow beard was propped at the top of the short companionway ladder. He held up a whisky bottle invitingly. When they did not respond he put it to his lips and swallowed greedily. When he paused to speak, his voice was harsh and shaky. 'Plenty more – better had be – down below.'

Lyttleton said, 'We're making enquiries, sir, about a child who went missing this morning.'

'Huh?'

'Little girl, wearing a blue anorak.'

'Relation of yours?'

Lyttleton tensed. 'What makes you ask that?'

'Oh, I dunno. All look the same to me, you lot.'

Lyttleton held out the photograph with which they had all been hurriedly issued.

'It's very muzzy.' The picture was indeed blurred, rushed through as it had been; but no more muzzy than the boat owner himself. As he leaned forward to get things in focus he lurched and almost fell overboard. 'No sea legs,' he mumbled. 'Not as young as I was.' He made a great effort, and all at once said clearly: 'Wearing a tartan skirt, wasn't she?'

Carver heard Abe Lyttleton's gasp, and moved in closer.

'What was that, sir?'

'That little girl, you booby. Black Watch. My old regiment. Awful lot of people seem to go round wearing it these days. Don't know where they think they've got the right . . .'

'I wonder if you would mind accompanying us to the station, sir? You could be most helpful.'

'Could I, now?' Under shaggy eyebrows there was a gleam of cunning. 'Anything there to wet my whistle, eh? Something to stop the old throat seizing up?'

He asked it again when he was sitting in the interview room, opposite DI Galloway.

'Coffee, that's all,' said Galloway curtly. 'Now, you remember this little girl was wearing a Black Watch tartan skirt, right?'

'Mm. Mmm, mmph.'

'And you saw her this morning?'

The boat owner appeared to be in danger of falling asleep. 'Isn't it tomorrow yet?'

'Not quite. Now, did you see her this morning?'

'That's what I told your two flat-footed friends. 'Course I saw her.'

'Good. Was she with anyone?'

A plastic cup of coffee was set in front of the witness. He peered unenthusiastically into it.

'Listen.' Galloway tried to keep his impatience in check. 'This is very important. That child's life could be in danger.'

'Can't I have a drink?'

'Only that. Now, please. You must be able to remember. Was the child on her own, or was she with somebody?'

The man gave a despairing tug at his beard, muttered into it, and surrendered. 'Well, I'm not sure if she was with anyone all the time. I mean, I don't know how long they'd been together.'

'They?'

'Her and this woman.'

'A woman?' said Galloway. 'Not a man?'

'Can't tell the difference sometimes, can you? These days, you never know. But this was a woman all right. Spotted coat. Might be leopard, or something.'

Four

It was well after dark when they began to cut down on some of the operations. The loudspeaker van touring the Riverdale estate and a neighbouring shopping area was recalled. Radio appeals continued to bring in a number of phone calls, none of them apparent hoaxes but none even remotely helpful. The door-to-door enquiries were suspended because there were precious few doors left to knock at. It hurt to mark time, now that the matter was clearly more serious than just a kid playing truant. Darkness was here, she had not come home, and it did not look as if she would do so now. So it was abduction – by a woman? Better than by a man. Or was it?

Perhaps during the night there would be a message from Margate or Brighton. Meanwhile patrols on night duty were ordered to intensify routine examinations of every alley and dustbin, every half-open door or splintered fence. But the ordinary public, the people who must sooner or later come up with a shred of useful memory, were by now mostly watching a late-night horror movie, or asleep.

Was Samantha Welsh asleep, or awake in terror?

First thing next morning, motorists over a wider and wider network of streets were stopped and asked if they had seen a little girl at this same time yesterday. Lyttleton, Muswell, Carver and Viv Martella had got so used to reeling off the description that they could probably have mouthed it in their sleep; would probably do just that for several nights to come. Divers tried another overgrown cut. A line of policemen fanned out over tracts of wasteland between dock buildings.

The radio again interrupted its music in homes and in cars stuck in traffic jams on the way to work. 'Black Watch type of skirt, white socks and brown sandal-type shoes. If anyone has any information, will they please contact the incident room at Sun Hill police station. The number to ring . . .'

Roy Galloway sat in his office, fuming and impotent. He had already spent half an hour pacing about, hovering irritably near the switchboard, and having another talk with the boat owner. There was nothing more to come from that source. Galloway sent the dismally sobered-up man back to his vessel after a breakfast more solid than he was used to.

The calls began to come in again, from Paddington and Bexleyheath and Greenwich. Some of them made you wonder what point there was in giving out detailed descriptions: sightings were reported of a Chinese girl in a black raincoat, a toddler with glasses, a couple of twins lost outside a Clerkenwell convenience.

Something fidgeted in Galloway's mind. It was not anything even as solid as a hunch. Perhaps it was no more than a reflex action. There had to be action of *some* kind, and moving the pieces around on the board was better than sitting still and waiting for someone else to come up with a gambit.

He wanted WPC Ackland to go and have another word with Theresa O'Brien.

June Ackland phoned the headmaster, to learn that Theresa had not shown up at school this morning.

'Don't say *she's* been abducted.' It was too grotesque. Even the weirdest pervert rarely went in for collecting them two at a time.

June got the O'Briens' address from the school and drove there fast, half expecting to be confronted by another distraught pair of parents. The door was cautiously opened to her by Theresa. One glimpse of the policewoman's uniform, and she tried to close it again.

June put her foot in the opening. 'Hello. I came to see why you're not at school.'

Theresa clung to the door handle, looking down at her feet with that evasive expression with which June was becoming all too familiar.

'Mum or dad in?' she asked as lightly as possible.

Theresa shook her head.

'Oh. So they don't know you didn't go to school?' When there was no reply she went on more aggressively: 'Come on now, Theresa. Are you scared of something?'

'No.' It was little more than a whisper, and an unconvincing one at that.

'Why were you scared to go to school? Did you tell a fib?' Now June was really angry. 'Theresa, did you make up all that nasty stuff? All that stuff about that man? *Did* you?'

Theresa's face dissolved into tears. She coughed out a little whining noise and with an abrupt wild shove got June's foot out of the way and slammed the door. June rang the bell again. She could see the girl's shadowy outline through the glass panel, but Theresa was not moving, just standing there mute.

It would not look too good to break down that door and upset the child still further.

Back at the nick, she was in time to hear Sergeant Cryer taking a call from the Brighton police. They had picked up Terence Lowe. Cryer beamed, promised someone would come and fetch him, and grabbed the internal phone to report the good news to Roy Galloway. Only maybe it was no longer the good news they might once have considered it to be. June waited for Galloway to come down and join them, and said: 'The O'Brien kid was at home.'

'Thank God for that. But why – '

'She didn't admit it outright, but I'm positive she's been lying. All that stuff about the flasher – she's been watching too much telly, if you ask me. It was invented. You could see it written all over her face.'

'You're positive?' Cryer snapped.

'Sarge, I know we still have to go on chasing up every possibility, but I'd swear this one's a non-starter.'

Galloway let out a shuddering breath. 'So it looks as if our little friend from Woodclose has been leading us up the garden path. The bloke we've been chasing after never existed?'

'Looks like it. Really, sir, I could be wrong, but – '

'I believe you,' said Galloway.

'You know something?' said Cryer wearily. 'I bet that kid's making sand castles on Margate beach right now. Any minute we'll get a phone call saying she's been taken in and given an ice cream and please will we come and collect her. Quite a little shuttle service we're running today.'

'Sarge.' Yorkie Smith, at the switchboard, indicated the phone on the nearest desk.

The call was not from Margate but from a small supermarket on the far side of Riverdale estate. The assistant had something to report about the little girl they had been hearing about on the radio – and about a woman who had been with her.

'A woman?' said Cryer. They all held their breath as he waited for more details. Then he looked across the desk and repeated slowly: 'In a leopard-skin mac. Yes, oh yes. We'll get someone over to the shop right away. And thank you very much indeed.'

Galloway said: 'So that old dipso wasn't just seeing things. I think I'll go and follow this one up. Address, Bob? Oh, and Ackland – you ought to be in on it, too. Let's go.'

The shop had a vast stock of goods crammed in on its shelves, behind glass under the counter, and piled up along the floor. It seemed to cater for every possible need on the estate: cans of food, a refrigerator full of fruit juices, rows of cigarette packets and sweets, teddy bears, jigsaw puzzles, newspapers and magazines, a rack of paperbacks, birthday cards, and coloured picture postcards of Tower Bridge and the Prince and Princess of Wales.

Galloway showed the girl behind the counter a picture of Samantha Welsh.

She nodded at once. 'Yes, that's her all right. And she was wearing a blue anorak and that tartan, like they said.'

'And the woman? Can you describe her a bit more?'

'Well, sort of fair hair. Touched up quite a bit, I'd say. And wearing that mac, leopard spots, sort of.'

'Does she shop here often?'

'Can't say I've noticed her before. Unless she comes in when

I'm off work – you could ask the boss, but he won't be in till this afternoon.'

'What did she buy?'

'Some food. Cakes, and a tub of ice cream. And a bottle of wine. Oh, and a bag of flour. And one of those little teddy bears, and a colouring book and some felt tips for the kid.'

'And the kid was all right?'

The assistant shrugged. 'Yeah.'

'Yeah?' Galloway echoed doubtfully.

'Well, I dunno, do I? I mean, I didn't take that much notice. You don't when you're serving a customer, you just serve them, and – '

'All right, all right.'

'Seemed happy enough so far's I could tell,' said the girl placatingly. 'I mean, nothing like a few presents, is there?'

Galloway silently consulted June Ackland. Where did they go from here? They were so close; there had to be a way of clinching it.

Off the cuff he asked: 'How did she pay?'

'Credit card.'

June Ackland smiled. Galloway felt a smile of his own coming all the way from deep inside. It was even better when the girl produced the counterfoil. A Smith or a Jones might have slowed things down a bit. But a name like Lubaczewska would surely not take too much locating.

'Have you got a phone book?'

There was no Lubaczewska in the area directory. From the car he called Sun Hill and spelled the name out carefully to Bob Cryer. The response came more quickly than he would have dared hope.

'Bit of luck, Roy. Yorkie Smith had dealings with a woman of that name just under a year ago. Married a Polish bloke who got killed in a hit and run. Yorkie was the one who had to go round and tell her, so it sticks in his mind. Number 5 Pickford Crescent, right?'

Galloway drove at a speed which made June Ackland cast two or three sidelong glances at him. With any other man she might have thought he was trying to impress her. But Galloway was not the one to waste time impressing anybody. His mind was fiercely concentrated on reaching their destination as fast as possible just in case . . .

Neither of them wanted to pursue that 'just in case'.

June hazarded: 'She wouldn't have bought a colouring book for the kid if anything was . . . well, going to happen. Would she? I mean, why?'

They reached Pickford Crescent. Seeing the turn-off a few seconds too late, Galloway jammed on his brakes and backed screechingly up the side road.

'Number 5.' He was willing it to be the right address and the right conclusion.

The door was opened by a woman with a pale, narrow face whose bone structure preserved its beauty in spite of the melancholy in her eyes.

'Mrs Lubaczewska?'

'Yes.' The woman's oddly oblique, wide eyes widened even more as she saw the uniformed WPC Ackland behind him.

'I'm Detective Inspector Galloway. We're making enquiries into the – '

She tried to close the door, yelling 'No!' as June flung herself along the narrow passage to the kitchen at the back of the flat. 'No, please.' Tears sprang to her eyes and she stumbled aside and clung to the kitchen door as Galloway followed June Ackland. 'We're only having a tea party.'

Samantha Welsh was perched on a stool, contentedly rolling pastry. Her face was pallid with flour and there was a dab of jam in one corner of her mouth. She smiled at the three of them, puzzled by the intrusion but unworried.

June said: 'Samantha, we've come to take you home.'

In the cool and clinical atmosphere of the interview room Galloway said: 'You were widowed last year, I'm told?'

'Yes.'

'Any kids of your own?' When Mrs Lubaczewska shook her head he probed: 'What made you pick her?'

'I . . . I thought she was lost.'

'On her way to school?' he said sceptically.

'But she wasn't going to school, not when I saw her.'

'How could you tell where she was going?'

'She was by the boats. Not going anywhere. Just watching the boats.'

'That was the first time you saw her?'

'At the dock,' Mrs Lubaczewska said dreamily. 'I like the docks. Especially in the summer. There are people to talk to.' Her eyes clouded over. 'Families,' she murmured.

The door opened. 'Oh, sorry, guv.'

'What is it, Ted?'

'Hammond, we're still holding him. The way things are now, wouldn't it be – '

'Let him go.' Galloway turned sympathetically back to the woman at the table. 'Look, the way I see it, you didn't mean any harm. But you must have known it was wrong. I mean, what about the kid's parents? They must have been worried sick, and there you were setting up little treats and parties and tucking her up in bed and all the rest of it. Didn't you ever think of the mother and father?'

'She never said anything about them.'

'Nothing?'

Her lips trembled, but she was not looking at him and no longer really hearing. Her misery came from the pain of loss, not from any awareness of wrongdoing or the existence of anybody else. As far as she was concerned, Samantha's parents had never existed.

Galloway wanted to be done with the emotionalism of it all. The facts had been verified; personal reverberations were none of his business. He was glad it was Ackland who had to hand the kid over, not himself. Tearfully ecstatic reunions, brimming over with a whole lot more emotion, were not his line.

June Ackland felt differently. She had gone through the bad bits, and now there was going to be the good bit. She looked forward to it. It was the sort of thing that made the job worthwhile. Holding Samantha's hand, she said: 'They won't half be pleased to see you.'

Samantha was silent and subdued. In her other hand she clutched the painting book, refusing to have it put in her school satchel or even to let go of it for a moment.

They went up in the lift and along the landing which June associated with bad news or depressing lack of news. Only now it was going to be a different story. There really were happy endings, every now and then.

She rang the bell and waited, smiling.

Mrs Welsh opened the door. She stared, then grabbed at Samantha.

'Sammy! What did I tell you, what *did* I . . .?'

Samantha was dragged from June's grasp and thrown against the wall. She cried out just once before her mother, holding her with one hand, began to beat her about the head with the other.

Welsh came pounding along the passage. 'What d'you think you're doing, you stupid bitch?'

'Don't you call me bleeding names.'

June tried to say something but was drowned out by Welsh. 'You don't have to belt her about like that, you shouldn't, she –'

'She may well deserve it, thank you very much.'

'What d'you . . .?'

The rest was lost as Mrs Welsh, fiercely active in her rage, kicked the door shut. June crumpled against the outside wall, putting her hand across her eyes to stop them blinking. Her fingers tightened across her forehead. Inside the flat the thudding went on, and now Samantha was beginning to scream.

June suppressed a sob in her throat. All in the day's work. That's what she would be told if she lodged a complaint.

She headed for the lift.

'And now,' said Galloway, 'let's get back to the real villains. Ted, you and Mike get back on the job. Go and relieve Chris and Jim on Queen's Parade.'

'You're not still banking on that one, guv?'

'Banking might be the right word, Ted. Off you go.'

'I still get a creepy feeling you've been fed a – '

'Creep off, Ted. At the double.'

Roach bit back whatever it was he had it in mind to say, and went downstairs. Galloway followed after a few minutes to check that Mrs Lubaczewska had read over her statement and signed it. He found the front office in uproar. Tom Penny and Bob Cryer were slanging each other and then taking it in turns to bellow accusations first at Hollis and then at Taffy Edwards.

'I'll have somebody's guts for garters,' Cryer was raging. 'We get through all that mess, everything out of order and now, on top of that, when we're supposed to be back to normal you . . . look, Tom, why the hell didn't you – '

'I gave the instructions,' retorted Penny, 'clearly enough. If some imbecile didn't pay attention to perfectly clear orders – '

'Nice and peaceful in here this morning,' observed Galloway. 'What's up?'

'The recharge unit's been out all night.'

'You mean, after all that switch-off chaos, nobody had the sense to switch on again?'

'We mean,' said Cryer, 'that all the radios over there are flat. And the ones that have been taken out on patrol must be just as flat, or with only a flicker left in them. So how the hell do we get in touch with anybody out there?'

'You'll just have to shout louder,' suggested Galloway.

He sorted out the last sad little details on Mrs Lubaczewska, and went back to his office for a call to the bank manager. No, there had been no apparent developments. No suspicious moves, or anyone showing any signs of acting strangely in or around the bank. Was the detective inspector quite sure . . .?

Yes, in his own mind Galloway was quite sure. He was in no mood for doubts from Roach or the bank manager. Conga would have had no reason to feed him a load of lies – not if he expected to grab any reward, he wouldn't.

Towards the end of the morning Bob Cryer came into the office without knocking, and without preamble said: 'And what the hell are your lot doing along Queen's Parade without notifying us?'

Galloway gripped the edge of his desk. 'What do you know about Queen's Parade?'

'Only that Ted Roach has been on his car radio yelling his head off.'

'Why? What's gone wrong?'

He listened with mounting incredulity and fury as Bob Cryer spat it out.

Roach was clamouring for help. On an obbo job, he said, at Queen's Parade – and two bloody great flatfoots were about to blow the whole game. Couldn't somebody make contact and pull them out, quick? There they were, Carver and Lyttleton, prowling round a Ford transit and making themselves conspicuous enough to frighten anybody off. From which Cryer assumed that the eager-beaver Jimmy Carver had rediscovered that transit where he had first spotted it, dodgy numberplate and tax disc and all, and was aiming to make a collar. Fair enough. But Roach wanted the two of them out of the way.

'So why don't you *get* them out of the way?' shouted Roy Galloway.

'Because their PR units are quite u.s., that's why. Dead. They can't hear us.'

'Your bloody great big clumsy woodentops – do you realize they're going to cock up a whole operation? What are you going to do about it? How are you going to get yourselves out of this bloody criminal mess you've made?'

'In the first place,' said Cryer, 'I've told your Ted Roach that we can't contact our two men, can't call 'em off, and he'll have to take whatever measures he thinks fit. And in the second place,' he said lethally, 'when it comes to a question of a cock-up, there wouldn't have been any such thing if you'd seen fit to put us in the picture.'

Galloway was seeing red. He had been so sure of making a killing, and now it was slipping through his fingers. 'Your mob has messed this up good and proper, Robert. There'll be hell to pay over this, I promise you.'

'Us? *We* messed it up? Now look here – '

'One more day,' ranted Galloway. 'That's all I needed, just

one more day. It just *had* to be this weekend.'

'If you choose not to notify the uniformed branch of what you're up to, don't blame them for carrying out the duties they're supposed to be on. If you don't want your toes trodden on, at least give us some idea where you're planting those precious toes. Right now, inspector, if I read the tea leaves aright, the only thing you'll get out of whatever it is you're tailing will be a bent tax disc.'

Galloway thought feverishly of his next possible move. Before he could make any move at all, the message was relayed from downstairs, in the most formal language, that due to circumstances beyond their control Detective Sergeant Roach and Detective Constable Dashwood had been forced to move in and take two suspects into custody.

Two suspects and not much else, Roach reported when he got back to Sun Hill. Unless you counted some new shelving in the basement of the boarded-up shop, some rough-and-ready plastering and a built-in cupboard. It looked like a cheap refurbishing job being rushed through for the reopening of the shop. Nobody had been digging. No sign of tunnels or subterranean access to the bank vaults.

Galloway kept Roach standing there in front of the desk while he sat back, let the adrenalin really get circulating, and treated himself at last to a full-scale explosion. 'I just don't believe it. One more day, and we'd have had all we needed on them. I swear it.'

'I don't think so,' said Roach stubbornly. 'Looks like your snout gave you a bummer.'

'No chance. What d'you take me for? How the hell you and Dashwood could let a pair of flaming woodentops step in and blow it, I . . . no, I just don't believe it. I don't see it. A cock-up like that – '

'It was your cock-up, sir.' Roach was flushed and furious, the high colour in his cheeks getting higher and brighter. 'You run around shouting your head off and thinking you can lay down the law all on your own.'

'Ted – '

'Just who the bloody hell do you think you are?'

'I'm your governor, that's who I am.'

'Is that a fact? Well, let me tell you something, *guv'nor*. It's about time you learned a few home truths.'

'One more word from you, sergeant, and I'll have you on a report.'

'I don't give a monkey's what you have me on. Not any more. You have me up on whatever you like, sir. You cocked it up, not me. Not me, not Mike, and certainly not the boys in uniform. You wouldn't listen, you don't want to listen, you don't want to know.'

'Right.' Galloway was almost glad to have someone to take it all out on. Roach was for it this time. 'That does it,' he said.

'And you know something? You used to be a good copper. A bit on the flash side, but good. Now you're no more than a loud-mouthed bully-boy who stamps his feet when he doesn't get everything all his own way. You don't have a monopoly on being right, sir, whatever your rank.'

'Get out.'

Roach got out.

Roy Galloway sat gripping the arms of his chair as the denunciations built up in his mind and he framed just how he was going to word the final damning accusation against Roach. This time it had gone too far. This time Ted Roach was for the chop.

He felt sick: sick because of things going so wrong, and sick because of letting things reach this stage with Roach. There was no way he could back down now and still maintain respect.

Conga hadn't fed him a bummer. There was no way he was going to believe that. Whatever cover-ups Roach attempted, whatever rotten rubbish Bob Cryer spewed up about radios on the blink, woodentops on the plod, it made no difference: the truth was that he had been in reach of a great collar, and the rest of them had made a pig's ear out of it.

He was tired, hungry, thirsty. If he sat here at this desk five minutes longer, he'd start thinking about the divorce again and feeling sorry for himself, and counting back over the years and finding himself face to face with somebody else who'd had it in for him and would never listen to reason.

He went down Sun Hill to the corner pub.

Bob Cryer and Ted Roach were sitting at the far end of the bar. It was all too obvious that Roach had been bending Cryer's ear. Automatically Galloway drifted towards them; then stopped, and hauled himself on to a stool a good ten feet away.

Sadie, the barmaid, was saying: 'Hey, Bob, that bank job was a bit cheeky, wasn't it?'

Galloway felt a chill. He looked round. The door was shut, the artificial flames danced in the gas fire. He tried to stop himself twitching.

'What bank?' asked Cryer.

'Glasscock Street. Just been on the news.'

Ted Roach leaned across the bar, glum but responding instinctively to any hint of evildoing. 'Glasscock Street?'

'Reckon they must have been down there for days, and nobody any the wiser.'

'First we've heard of it,' said Cryer.

'Only dug right under the road, didn't they? Straight up the sewer, right into the vault.'

'I knew it,' said Roach very audibly to Cryer. 'I told him his snout sold him one.'

'Oh, I doubt it, Ted. Glasscock Street's not even on our ground.'

'Only just over the boundary. And don't tell me they wouldn't have been glad of a nice little diversion. Left them in peace to get on with things.'

Galloway's mouth was dry. He said harshly: 'Scotch, please.'

'Sorry, Roy. Didn't see you come in.' Sadie reached for a glass and swept it expertly up to the optic. 'Hey, you heard about – '

'Yes, I heard you.'

'Somebody dropped a clanger?'

Galloway looked along the bar. 'And whatever they're having along there.'

Bob Cryer favoured him with a dour half-smile, but pushed his glass forward. Ted Roach sat mute, refusing to turn his head.

'The usual, Ted?' said Sadie.

It was an almost imperceptible nod.

Galloway edged closer. 'Haven't been that bad, have I?'

It was Cryer who took it on himself to answer. 'Yes. Worse.'

They drank. Galloway's whisky took only a few seconds to go down. With an effort he said: 'Right, then. See you later, back at the nick ... Ted. We'll go through everything we've got. Together. Straighten it out. Okay?'

Roach was still not looking at him. 'Okay, guv.'

'I'll see you.'

'See you, Roy,' said Cryer, into an infinity stretching behind the shelf of spirits.

Five

Some of the hard cases you had to deal with were often no better than animals. Animals: it had become a useful shorthand to describe a lot of them. The trouble was, a policeman's lot did not just involve human animals. Over the months and years Sun Hill officers had been caught up in the problems of several four-legged ones, not to mention a selection of birds, from parrots to thieving magpies. Yorkie Smith, on point duty, had once stuck out his arm to find it embracing a leg of lamb which had literally fallen off the back of a lorry. Valuable hours had been spent dealing with a rampaging goat which proved to have got high on cannabis growing wild among the weeds in a back garden. And now, right at the beginning of a working day, there was another matter of four-footed strays.

'Two of our pigs,' said a Mr Roger Philpot on the phone, 'are missing.'

WPC Martella repeated the message over her shoulder to Sergeant Cryer. He stared, suspecting a hoax. 'Since when did we have pigs on this manor?'

'Ask some of our admirers,' offered Muswell.

'The City Farm,' said Viv Martella. 'A break-in.'

Cryer checked the wall map. Taffy Edwards ought to be somewhere in the vicinity of that patch of green, most likely sneaking a second breakfast in that favourite café of his.

He sucked his lips in. On the whole they had a pretty good team here. Jimmy Carver, at first so soggy behind the ears, had settled in well. The newcomer, Abe Lyttleton, might not have made a go of his previous two postings but so far showed every sign of pulling his weight at Sun Hill. Yorkie Smith was a bit of a bouncing yokel in some ways, but utterly reliable. Hollis would always be a moaner, with an assortment of pains adding up to one great pain in the neck; but at least he had a knack with paperwork. Muswell . . . oh, Muswell was a sight too greedy, piling up the overtime during that miners' strike, and Cryer would not have put it past him to go moonlighting in off-duty hours – only God help him if it was ever proved. But in his own heavy way he was tough and resourceful.

As for the girls, Viv Martella looked too sleek and sultry to be a serious copper. It was a misleading impression, as many a petty crook had found to his cost. And June Ackland was . . . well, there was something about that slim, trim figure of hers and about . . . Cryer stopped himself. Talk about racism in the station: if they had known what he was thinking, there'd be a right royal outcry about sexism.

And so Cryer came back to PC Edwards. Getting slack. Too much time fretting about his days off and whether he could catch this or that train to North Wales; and too much time scrounging meals in that café, skiving on the job, waiting for radio instructions instead of pacing the beat to stop things before they happened.

Martella took another call at the switchboard. A man was ringing in about a pig trampling all over the back alley behind the bus station.

'Not far from Taffy's nosh bar,' observed Cryer. 'Get him out there. Keep the thing cornered, and we'll see about picking it up.'

They notified Mr Philpot, who sounded pleased, but not eager enough to go and collect his animal. The Land Rover was in for repair, he explained, and the only vehicle he had available was a Mini. And where, he demanded ungratefully, was the second pig?

'All right,' sighed Cryer. 'Who've we got? Muswell, you get out there in the Sherpa and I'll get Carver to meet you at' – his finger traced a route across a segment of the map – 'Pound Place.'

'The Sherpa's loaded up, sarge.'

'Well, get it unloaded. And hurry up.' Leaning over the

switchboard, Cryer said: 'Get Jimmy for me. He's good with kids, he's probably good with animals.'

'Yeah, well,' protested Muswell, 'if it shits all over the van I'm not cleaning it out.'

'Oh yes, you are.'

As Muswell left, Hollis said: 'Rather them than me, sarge. Pigs can get very nasty, you know.' He swung his shoulders from side to side, and winced.

'Agony, is it, Reg?'

'Just catches me now and again, sarge,' said Hollis gallantly.

Martella glanced back at him. 'Only a prize wally would have hurt himself on a field training course.'

'Look, if I'd wanted to do PT I'd have joined the SAS, wouldn't I?'

'Yeah. He who dares, ricks his back.'

'Wait till they send the rest of you on it. It'll cripple half the Force.'

'Have you been to see the CMO recently?' Cryer demanded.

'Well, not since that time when he said I was to stay on light duties until – '

'I reckon it's time you had it checked again. A full physical. You never know, there might be something really wrong with you.'

'Look, sarge, I'm not swinging the lead,' said Hollis plaintively.

'Well, let's find out. Because if there's something wrong with you, you're no good to me and I'm getting you transferred.'

Hollis looked interested, vaguely hopeful. 'What, a job upstairs?'

'Yes. We'll have a lift put in.' Cryer turned his attention to the PR message coming in. 'You got that porker in your sights yet, Edwards?'

Taffy Edwards had in fact succeeded in cornering the pig, but was none too confident of his ability to hold out all that long. The animal was rooting contentedly along the cobbled alley, having overturned a dustbin and helped itself to the more savoury morsels, leaving the rest of the rubbish spread across the gutter. When it had finished, it was just as likely to charge out of the alley at the speed with which it had charged in. Taffy crouched in a position suggesting something halfway between a lion-tamer's coaxing stance and a bull-fighter's poised readiness.

'About bloody time,' he greeted the Sherpa as it came to a halt across the end of the alley.

The appreciative crowd of bystanders increased as Muswell and Carver joined Edwards. Jimmy Carver was self-consciously carrying a metal lasso, brought from the dog-handler's store, which looked more likely to inflict damage on the gaping audience than to snare the pig with brisk efficiency.

'Go on, Jimbo,' Muswell encouraged him. 'Get in there.'

'Pig,' said Carver entreatingly. 'Come on, piggy. Pig . . . pig . . .'

Their quarry grunted, and buried its snout in a stodgy mess of squashed food cartons. A few members of the crowd cheered it on.

'Take it easy.' Carver made a tentative jab with the metal ring, which the pig headed contemptuously aside. 'Hey, steady now. Steady.'

Muswell snorted almost as raucously as the animal. 'Go on, you great girl's blouse!'

Goaded, Carver made a wild lunge and at last succeeded in getting the metal round the pig's neck. It lashed out with its hind legs, but slithered on the débris and landed up against the wall, squealing in rage.

Muswell looked back at the van.

'How we going to get it in there?'

'I don't . . .' Carver braced himself to keep his captive pinned against the wall. 'Look, that old door over there. On that tip at the end. Drag it out as a ramp or something.'

Together Muswell and Edwards hauled the door into place, and waved to Carver to bring his animal-training act to a triumphant conclusion. Half dragging, half steering the pig towards the van, he managed to get it to the foot of the ramp. It squealed and tried to lunge to the left. Members of the crowd scattered, regrouped, and cheered again. Muswell and Edwards closed in to either side, while Carver did not so much urge the pig into the van's interior as let it drag him along with it. When he had backed quickly out and Edwards had slammed the doors shut, Jimmy Carver said with some pride: 'Right, that's it. Over to you.'

'Yes, you can stop playing with your pet now. Back to the beat and some real work, eh?'

Carver paced off, not knowing whether the round of applause offered by the onlookers was genuine or ironic.

Muswell and Edwards drove to the City Farm, with their passenger thudding and honking a protest behind them. The farm was an unexpected little oasis at the end of a suburban street, with more rows of semi-detached houses on its far side. Roger Philpot was waiting for them, congratulatory but still slightly peevish about the absence of the second pig. Shepherding his retrieved animal towards its sty, he identified it. 'This is Plonk. So Pickle's still at large.'

'No sweat,' said Muswell. 'We'll put it out on all units. What's its reg number?' Then hastily, seeing that this had not gone down too well, he peered inside the van, wrinkled his nose, and added: 'You got a hose, sir? Taffy, go get the hose.'

'Oh, no, mate. You're the driver.'

'What are you moaning about? I thought you was brought up on a farm?'

'Yes, boyo. Welsh woollies, not English pigs. Now, Mr Philpot, we've not yet established how – '

'This has really thrown my egg deliveries this morning. Hold these for me, would you?' As if by magic a cardboard tray of eggs was put into Taffy's hands.

'Mr Philpot, please. We still have no idea how the pigs escaped. You talked about a break-in.'

'And that's what it was. No escape. Somebody let them out, deliberately. Come and look.'

Still balancing the tray of eggs, Edwards accompanied the farmer round the end of the sty to a stretch of wire fencing.

Philpot indicated a large ragged gash in the fence.

'The sty door had been opened,' he said. 'And as to the fence – well, pigs don't use wire cutters.'

'Vandals?'

'Animal Life League, I think. We've had a few letters lately – "Meat is murder," that kind of thing. You're not a vegetarian, are you?'

'Oh no, I'm Welsh, I eat anything.'

A flock of geese stormed across the path as they walked back. Edwards picked his way warily around the rackety gaggle and took the opportunity of handing the tray of eggs back to its owner.

'Pickle's still missing,' Philpot remarked with a heavy hint of accusation. 'You may not think it all that serious, but she's a very important member of our community.'

'It's not a question of what *I* think, sir. But we'll do all we can, depend on that.' Returning to the Sherpa, he walked round the side of the van to the open rear doors. 'You finished yet, Muzz?'

From inside came a last swish of stinking liquid as Muswell swept it vigorously out into the open. 'Gardez-loo! Oops.' He grinned down at the speckled mess over Taffy's trousers. 'All done, then?'

'No mate, you missed the top half.'

Muswell's lips twisted into false commiseration. 'Want a lift back to your beat?'

'Oh, thanks very much. You might at least say sorry.'

'Good stuff, that. Makes your toes curl.' Muswell shook the brush in the fresh air. 'How'd they get out, then?'

'The nutty brigade cut a hole in the fence. Least, that's what he reckons. Anyway, there's naff-all to go on.'

'Right. Let's leave it. Where do you want dropping off?'

'Larry's. I could do with a cup of tea.'

Edwards climbed into the van. Muswell, reaching for the ignition, said: 'Phew. Stick your feet outside, won't you?'

Taffy unbuttoned his jacket and flapped it in defiance.

Muswell drove fast, with the windows open, in a hurry to

ditch him outside the café known to every man on this beat – better known to some than others.

'Not another breakfast already, Taff?' Larry, fat and hospitable in a greasy vest adorned with the splashes of a dozen earlier breakfasts, propped his top-heaviness against the counter.

'Elevenses,' said Edwards.

'What you been doing, then?'

'Arresting a pig, as it happens.'

'Saved a few rashers for us?'

'No, Larry. Look, I just want a cup of tea.' As Larry trundled behind the counter and stimulated the large urn into uttering a fine hiss of activity, he said: 'Here, you haven't got another runaway pig on the premises, have you?'

'Can't oblige, sorry. Plenty of dead flies, though.'

Taffy Edwards looked at the contents of an ashtray, the sandwiches in the glass case on the counter, and the consistency of the tea in his cup, and was prepared to believe every word of that.

Henry Talbot made a circuit of the Sun Hill corridors with a small clutch of memoranda in his left hand. With his right hand he doled them out like a philanthropist distributing largesse to the poor and underprivileged. He looked grave yet well content. As the chief superintendent's clerk he derived a certain relish from handing over instructions which he knew would be unpopular but for which he could at any crucial moment disclaim responsibility. Not that Talbot invariably wished to disclaim such responsibility: indeed, he took considerable pleasure in framing the memoranda himself, watching the chief super sign them, and watching the faces of those who found themselves landed with the result.

'Bullshit!' was Ted Roach's immediate reaction.

New overtime restrictions were to be imposed. These must not, however, be allowed to impair operational effectiveness. Although paperwork might in certain unspecified circumstances get held up, everyone must endeavour to be as efficient as possible in the issue of reports to whichever department was involved.

Roach glowered up at Talbot. 'You've read this crap you're carting about?'

'I drafted it.'

'Paperwork is the only bloody thing that *doesn't* get held up round here.'

'Perhaps if your CID brethren were to clock in promptly, there'd be less need for overtime.' Talbot grimaced meaningly at the empty chair behind Dashwood's desk.

'Mike's out on a job.'

'He's not booked out on the duty state. Or in,' said Talbot puritanically as he left the room.

'Pedantic little twat!' Roach hurled after him.

In Galloway's office the phone began to ring. Roach hurried through and lifted the receiver. The caller's name meant nothing to him.

'Barry Blades? Sorry, mate, what – '

'Immigration.'

Before Roach could pursue this, Roy Galloway came in and held out his hand to take the call. 'Hello, Barry. Sorry I didn't get back to you yesterday. What time you going to be here? Half-past eleven, fine. Just see the duty sergeant if I'm not around, okay?'

'Immigration?' said Roach. 'And what would they be wanting of the likes of us?'

'Deporting the Irish. And you're first.'

Just to wipe the smile off his DI's face, Roach held out the memorandum which Talbot had delivered.

'Operational overtime?' Galloway read it out aloud. 'What's triggered all this off?'

'Maybe following up yesterday.'

'What yesterday?' Galloway looked round the office. 'And where's Mike?'

'Out checking on that con artist with the wardrobes. Checking on Miss Clark and the people who know her and who might have had a key to the flat.'

'Oh, that. Should have been wrapped up last night.'

'That's what I mean. The chief super told us no overtime, and Mike was on overtime, and not the only one. So now we get it all in writing.'

'Bloody ridiculous. Anyway, what are *you* up to this fine day, then?'

'That credit card job.'

'Any imminent danger of an arrest?' jibed Galloway. He went downstairs to arrange with Bob Cryer for Blades of Immigration to borrow three of his lads. Cryer was far from anxious to co-operate. He saw little reason why officers needed for nicking real villains should be commandeered to lean on a few poor sods who had been born in the wrong country and were now destined to be shipped back there. Routine policing encompassed enough dirty work of its own, without doing other people's dirty work for them. But in its way this too, officially, was routine. You had to go along with it, even when it turned your stomach.

PC Lyttleton was already on patrol in the area of the Caffrey Street sweatshop on which Blades had his eye. Carver and Muswell were detailed to take the van and join him at the junction with Commercial Street, following Blades and his sidekick in their car. The sidekick, Greg Swinton, was a quiet man but a deadly one: dark and withdrawn, he had the predatory look of a hunter who knew he could strike wherever he chose and always have the back-up of other officers' muscle.

Abe Lyttleton was waiting for them on the corner by a derelict chapel, its notice-board still holding shreds of waterlogged paper on which an indecipherable text had given up all hope of getting its message across. Muswell looked him up and down without favour. 'Hello, Snowball. You in on this?'

Blades, a dapper little man who made up for Swinton's shadowy introspection with a punchy intimation of going in and grabbing whatever there was to get without any argument, said: 'I want one of you at the front, one at the back, one in with us.' He stabbed a thumb at Lyttleton. 'You're the beat officer, right? So you'd best be the one inside. And remember, I'm not asking any of you to do anything. No rough stuff and no nonsense about acting on your own initiative, get it? You're just here to ensure there isn't a breach of the peace. Got that?'

They nodded morose assent.

Blades led the way down the street of decrepit brewery buildings split up into shabby factories and warehouses. Beside a door which could not have been repainted these past ten years was a notice-board advertising jobs available.

'We'll be doing the buggers a favour,' said Blades loudly. 'Most of em'd be better off back in Calcutta, anyway.'

Inside there was a whirr of machines. The floor creaked and thrummed under the pulse of the equipment, muffling the noise of the intruders' footsteps. An Indian in a shiny grey lounge suit saw them coming, and scuttled nervously from behind his glass partition.

'Mr Dev?' Blades expanded with the certainty of his own power. 'Immigration Department of the Home Office.'

'Yes,' said Mr Dev resignedly.

'I wonder if I could have a chat with some of your employees?'

Dev shrugged and stole a glance at Swinton, who had a glint of pleasurable anticipation in his eyes.

'Just the iffy ones, Greg,' said Blades. 'Straight down to the nick with 'em.'

Lyttleton stood a few paces back as Swinton approached a man stitching a jacket and began to talk quietly but incisively in Bengali. A white girl whose moist brow could well have illustrated the veracity of the term 'sweatshop' walked past, veering in close. 'Ain't you got nothing better to do?' Another appeared at Lyttleton's elbow. 'Leave the poor blighters alone.'

Blades was snapping his fingers for the passports of two dark, hunched women at one of the benches. When he had inspected them and found them in order, his expression was one of disgust rather than apology. 'Mrs Gupte and Mrs Chatterjee. Hm. There'll soon be more Chatterjees over here than Patels.'

He prowled round the room. Machines fell silent one after

another. Heads bowed or tilted sideways. Uneasy eyes studied him; and studied Swinton, making his own soft-footed circuit but always alert for a command from his boss.

Blades stopped beside a man with a steam iron, whose regular movements slowed to a halt.

'Him, I think.'

Swinton resumed the questioning. He nodded with a show of sympathy, but the broadening of his smile confirmed that he had made a kill. As the man's shoulders slumped, Swinton turned to Blades. There was no need for words. They knew one another by now.

As Lyttleton led the man downstairs, a West Indian near the door said: 'You proud of yourself, black man?'

Out in the street, Abe waited for the others to join him. He kept a hand lightly on the defeated immigrant's arm, but the man was too dejected to make a run for it. 'Thanks for your help, son.' Blades emerged, waiting for Carver to come round the corner and Muswell to bring up the rear. He included them all in his thanks. 'Cheers, then. Maybe see you lads back at the nick. Well done.'

Swinton opened the rear door of the car and waved their captive in.

Muswell sneered as they drove off. 'Well done, chaps,' he mimicked. His gaze fell unfavourably on Abe Lyttleton. 'Another blow against the black economy, eh?'

Somebody from a side door spat.

Lyttleton moved away. Behind him, Muswell, about to cross the road to the van, said: 'Oh, Snowball, how many times have I told you to use a hanky?'

'What?'

'You've got gob all down your back. Here, Jimbo, take him in hand. Clean him up and change his loincloth.'

As Muswell disappeared round the far side of the van, Carver dug out a paper tissue and dabbed at Lyttleton's shoulder. 'Right, there you go. Fancy a drink after work?'

'What's this?' Lyttleton was taut with anger. 'Your community relations bit?'

Carver stared. 'All right, then. Piss off.'

It was the sort of thing to leave a nasty taste in your mouth. Unless, of course, you were a Swinton or a Muswell. They would both enjoy a scene like that, each in his own way.

Animals . . .

Sun Hill had not yet had its full quota of animals. Even before the pig incident had been satisfactorily rounded off, and only seconds after Jimmy Carver had got back to the station, the phone was clamouring about another batch of wild creatures – dead ones this time. There was a disturbance at the fur shop in Masson Row, apparently set up by Animal Life demonstrators. There were three of them in the shop, refusing to budge, and a few more outside: mostly women, according to the report from Simeon Logue, the owner.

'Masson Row,' said Sergeant Cryer. 'Taffy's beat again. Seems to be cut out for the world of wildlife. And who else can we raise?' He scanned the map and the duty roster. 'Yes, call up June, she should be pretty adjacent. Carver, you get down there in the van and go in with them. And be careful how you handle it.'

'Handle what, sarge?'

'It's Nutters-for-Nature flag day, Jimbo,' said Muswell cheerfully.

'And you go with him.'

'But sarge, we don't need that many . . .'

Cryer's nose swung towards him like a weather vane heralding a storm. Muswell bent to the wind, and set off once more with Carver.

June Ackland had reached the scene ahead of them. She was standing well back along the pavement, sizing up the situation and waiting for reinforcements. There was no sign of Taffy Edwards.

Outside the shop a group squatting on the pavement kept chanting monotonously: 'Fur traders out . . . fur traders out . . .'

Muswell looked as if he was ready to enjoy himself for the

second time that day. 'You go at the dykes,' he said to June. 'We'll take the queers.'

'Fur traders out . . .'

Flanked by the two men, June edged her way into the shop. At the best of times there would be little space to spare in here. Right now the place was dominated by two women and a young man with long hair, drawn back into a wispy pigtail with a red ribbon. One of the women, dark-haired and determined, kept thrusting a leaflet at the shopkeeper. He snatched it from her and threw it over his shoulder. She began to wave another one to and fro in front of his face.

June reached the counter. 'Can I have a look at what you're handing out, please, madam?'

The woman ignored her and thrust the leaflet under Simeon Logue's nose yet again.

'I don't want to read your damned leaflet,' he yelled.

Carver and Muswell shouldered their way in. Muswell assumed his best official manner. 'Do you want these persons on your premises, sir?'

'Oh yes, they're very good for custom, very good for my business! Of course I don't want them on my premises. Or anywhere within a hundred miles.'

'Then we shall assist you to remove them.'

The young woman who had been flourishing the leaflet let herself crumple to the floor. She braced her feet against the counter. Obviously she had played this kind of drama before and knew how to be difficult. She was dressed in a black nylon blouse and skirt, and her hair and eyes were almost dark reflections of the clothes. She could have been attractive, if it were not for the shadowy gashes of impatience tugging the corners of her mouth down. She was well spoken, in a domineering way. 'We are only trying to put a point of view. Why do you have to come in here and – '

'Would you mind putting that point of view outside?' said Carver, bending to get his hands under her armpits.

'Yes, we do mind.'

'Now look, ladies – '

'Don't patronize us, you pig.' It was the other woman, getting one arm round a rack of furs. 'Fur traders out,' she began chanting again. 'Fur traders out.' The words were echoed by the supporters on the pavement outside.

'Either you leave under your own steam,' warned Muswell, 'or you get carried out.'

'Fur traders out!'

'Right. Let's clear the place.'

June Ackland made an abrupt swoop, dislodging the woman from the rack and throwing her neatly into Muswell's arms. He twisted her once and forced her out through the shop door. Jimmy Carver stooped to take over the dark woman more securely. She took some lifting. It was only when June came to his aid that they could heave her out to join her friends. The man was less trouble. He went on repeating their slogan in a thin voice but offered no resistance when Muswell came back in and bundled him towards the door.

In the doorway Carver said: 'Right, ladies, calm it. Anyone who tries to get back in gets nicked for a breach of the peace.'

'We'll do it again no matter how many times you lock us up.'

PC Edwards appeared on the fringe of the group just as the thin young man made an unexpected dive for the interior of the shop. Carver grabbed him.

'Better late than never, Taffy,' said Muswell.

'I only just got the call.'

'Oh, yeah?' Muswell went to open the back door of the van. The protesters were chanting yet again, but making no move to escape. They seemed to relish the idea of martyrdom. 'No point calling you while you was in Larry's, was there?'

'I wasn't in Larry's.'

'Breaking the habit of a lifetime.'

'I bloody wasn't.' Edwards turned his back on the protesters, who were beginning to look curiously at the two policemen. 'Look, I've been pounding the beat with pig shit on my trousers for the last two bloody hours because of you. Have you been dropping me in it with Cryer?' When Muswell ignored this and began urging one of the women towards the van, Taffy demanded: '*Have* you? Here, I'm bloody talking to you.'

'I don't need to, mate. He already knows you're a lazy git.'

Two of the group changed their tactics and tried to escape across the road, but were blocked by a slow-moving dustcart. The dark woman eyed the door of the shop as if contemplating a last defiant invasion. June Ackland and the other three closed in, herding them into the van like sheep. Made a change from pigs, anyway.

'Fur traders out!'

The raucous song went on and on as Muswell drove off towards Sun Hill.

Six

The newest housing estate near the main railway line was still a local showpiece. Tower blocks had ceased to be the favoured building style of housing authorities: tall monuments to misery, petty crime and ultimate dereliction, they thrust up from the fringes of the neighbourhood, but had made no inroads into the recent development. Town planners often made conducted tours of the tidy streets here, with their blocks of smart yellow-brick flats on a human scale and their trim little lawns. It was not suburbia, but it was not a potential slum. Or not yet, anyway.

Galloway did not like to comment aloud that even the criminals around here were smoother and more skilled than on other parts of the manor. The two ladies were already upset enough, and in no mood for flippant observations.

He looked from one smartly painted, unscratched front door to the other. The doors, like the window curtains and the narrow flowerbeds, were all of a piece with Mrs Dixon and Mrs Lambert and their remarkably unruffled hairdos. Nobody would smash down doors like those, or go at the residents with an iron bar. Everything here was neater and more subtle.

'These men delivering the wardrobe,' he recapped, 'knocked on your door at nine thirty. That's right, Mrs Dixon?'

Mrs Dixon plucked at the string of her pinafore, a spotless pattern of cornflowers matching the blue of her eyes. 'Two very nice polite men,' she said, as if to excuse them for whatever they might have done later. 'Mrs Lambert hadn't said she'd bought a new wardrobe, but she does buy lots of things from Bensham's, and ... well, they seemed so natural. And I always do let people in for Beryl when she's out. You know, meter readers, television repairers and so on.'

Yes, Galloway could see all that. It was all so pat, good-neighbourly, part of the atmosphere. A sensitive villain with a sensitive nose would have no difficulty in smelling out the possibilities.

'Do other people know you've got the key to Mrs Lambert's place?'

'Well, I suppose some people could. They see us going to and fro a lot.'

'Mm. So, you came along with the men delivering the wardrobe to Mrs Lambert's, and you let them in.'

'They could hardly leave it in the street.' Mrs Dixon's eyes began to sparkle with a hint of tears.

Her friend put out a consoling hand. 'Please, Marian, nobody's blaming you.' Where Mrs Dixon was fluffy and agitated, with a repetitive note of self-pity in her voice, Mrs Lambert was spare and decisive, the austere cut of her grey suit matching her pleasantly authoritative manner. 'Perhaps you had better come in and see for yourself, inspector.'

She led the way through an unnaturally tidy sitting room to a combined breakfast room and kitchen. There was not a smear on the work surfaces, no pan was out of place, you felt that nothing would ever dare let itself be disturbed. A faint aroma of perfumed sink cleaner hung in the air. In the bedroom things were almost as orderly, yet not quite. A few undergarments had been tossed on the bed: normal enough if the owner was in a hurry to get out, but not normal for anyone as meticulous as Mrs Lambert. And the dressing table was not merely tidy: it was bare.

'If only I'd looked round properly when I let them out!' wailed Mrs Dixon. 'But I had to keep out of their way when they were carrying it through – I mean, I do always stay somewhere inside when I let people in for Beryl, only I wasn't to *know* . . .'

Mrs Lambert contemplated the room with distaste. 'It's just knowing somebody's been in here.' She reached towards the door of a fitted cupboard.

Galloway said quickly: 'I'd be grateful if you didn't touch anything until our scenes of crime officer has had a chance to look things over.' He turned back to Mrs Dixon. 'Did they get you to sign a delivery note or anything like that?'

'Yes,' she said eagerly. 'So they did.'

'Now, the letterhead – did you notice any name printed on it?'

'I'm afraid I didn't.' Mrs Dixon was despondent again. 'They just said they were from Bensham's, and they had this wardrobe to deliver. They only took a few minutes to get it in. I had no reason to suspect anything.'

'And when did they come back?'

'Oh, not more than three-quarters of an hour later. And they were very apologetic and said they'd made a mistake, the wardrobe wasn't for Mrs Lambert after all.'

'So you let them back in, and they took the wardrobe away.'

'But they were only here for a few seconds. I don't see how they could have stolen anything. I mean, I was right outside the door, and they just got the wardrobe and moved it out.' She looked dismally at her friend. 'Oh, dear. Perhaps I didn't lock the door properly when I let them out.'

'I'm sure you did, Mrs Dixon,' said Galloway. 'I think there was a man in the wardrobe.'

Driving back to the station, he was filled with reluctant admiration for the perpetrators of this theft. It had to be the same lot who had hit the Clarks, which Mike Dashwood was checking out right now. So cocky it wasn't true: the wardrobe in both cases. Even reference to the same store, Bensham's. It was odds on that some bent bloke in their despatch department was supplying the right names and addresses.

Someone must have seen those jokers and their van. They had been lucky once, they couldn't be allowed to get away with it twice. As for them having a third go – no, that was not on. There had to be extensive local enquiries made this very day.

In his office he rang the chief superintendent's office. Henry Talbot answered and smoothly asked if he could take a message.

'Yes, you can. I want Mr Brownlow to authorize some overtime.'

'Does it come within the terms?'

It would have been good to send a message back along the line that would wrap itself round Talbot's officious neck and strangle him.

'It's for enquiries into a firm of villains whom we'll lose unless we get a decent lead today.'

'I think Mr Brownlow wanted to see you this afternoon in any case, sir. I'll speak to him as soon as he's free, and let you know.'

In the doorway Mike Dashwood suppressed a smirk. He knew the effect Talbot always had on the DI. Galloway flung at him: 'All right, Mike. *You'll* be the one on overtime when I've fixed it.'

The name of Henry Talbot cropped up at about the same time in the front office. Reg Hollis, sidling up to Bob Cryer, said: 'Sarge, I've heard a rumour that Henry Talbot's thinking of retiring.'

'That's right,' Cryer grunted. 'We're holding a piss-up for him in a telephone kiosk.'

'Yes, well. I mean, how d'you see me, I was sort of wondering, as the . . . er . . . next chief superintendent's clerk?'

Cryer looked him up and down. 'I can honestly say I can't think of anyone more suitable at Sun Hill.'

'Oh, thank you, sarge.'

'Petty,' contributed Viv Martella from the switchboard. 'Bloody-minded. Sneaky. Oh, it fits.'

'Hey, look here. You don't know a thing about it. It's not an easy job. You have to be able to handle responsibility, take the load off the chief super, advise him, know all the rules and regs. Right, sarge?'

'Right,' said Cryer. 'The only problem is, it's not a job for an able-bodied copper.'

Hollis hesitated only a fraction of a second. 'No, well, exactly. Er, I mean, I'm not one to complain, right, but I've been wondering about whether my back's been – well, permanently damaged.'

'Match your brain then, won't it?' said Martella.

A sound of singing seethed up again as the door to the cell block swung open. 'Four little pigs in blue, lads, four little pigs in blue . . .'

'Do we have to put up with that row, sarge?'

'Until the court tomorrow, we do. No way I could give that lot bail. Right, where's the charge sheet? Come on, Carver. You're the one in the thick of it.'

They went along the corridor, as the chanting took another turn. 'On and on and on and on . . .'

'In the charge room with 'em. Muswell around? And June's up in the canteen. Get her down.'

The protesters redoubled the volume of their anthem as PC Carver began to read out his statement. 'At ten o'clock this morning I and the other officers here present were called to Premier Furs, a clothing shop on Masson Row.'

'Big brave boys in blue,' said the dark woman, her eyes smouldering hotter with hatred by the moment.

'In the shop were three persons who the proprietor, Mr Logue, confirmed were unwanted on the premises. We therefore assisted him to eject them.'

As the chanting threatened to drown Carver's voice, Cryer suddenly blew his top. 'Shut up!'

There was a surprising hush.

Carver gulped and went on: 'The prisoners were arrested while attempting to continue occupying the shop, and forcibly to re-enter it when once removed. Such an attempt amounted, in my opinion, to threatening behaviour likely to cause a breach of the peace.'

'Breach of the peace?' said one of the men. 'There was no breach of the peace till you lot barged in.'

Cryer scraped a chair along the floor and sat down, facing the huddle of men and women who had been offered chairs but preferred sitting on the floor or propping themselves against the wall. 'You heard what the officer said. Anything sensible you want to add to that?'

'Yes. You're a lot of bastards.'

Cryer turned to the woman, the one with undoubted style and intelligence. At least they ought to be able to discuss things rationally. 'What about you?' he invited her.

'Only that we'll do it again and again until the murder stops.'

Cryer gave up. The intellectual idealists were always the trickiest to deal with. They were often more grief than bank robbers. He said wearily: 'In that case I'm afraid we're going to have to look after your property while you stay with us. Do you mind turning out your pockets, please?' He waited, saddened but unpetrified by the woman's stony stare. 'Could you turn out your pockets?'

The woman who was so assuredly the centrepiece of the whole demonstration said very slowly and deliberately: 'No, we could not.'

Cryer winced inside, but refused to show it. Maybe there were some coppers who fitted the stereotype and loved throwing their weight about and pushing their legal powers as far as they would go. He wasn't one of them. But now it had come to it. You knew when it got bad, and now it was really that bad. He said: 'Ackland, take this lady down to one of the cells and search her. Muswell, take that other one down – oh, and her as well – and get Martella to give a hand.'

Muswell beamed with delight. June Ackland's inviting lips thinned and were sucked in, repelled and far from inviting.

The cell allocated was cold and clinical, enough to deter anyone who fancied putting on a great big act. What point in an act when there was only a trained policewoman to observe it and cope with it? But the woman was tingling with a sort of icily feverish ecstasy. In some way – June could sense it, and hated the sensation – this meant more than the squatting on pavements and wailing slogans in a grotty little furrier's shop.

She slipped on the plastic gloves and said: 'Look, I'm sorry, but if you won't take things off then I have to do something about it.'

'Then you'll have to do it, won't you?' The woman watched the sheathed hands until June swung her round to face the wall. 'Do you enjoy degrading your fellow women?'

'All you have to do is agree that – '

'I don't agree with pigs. Or sows like you. Go ahead and enjoy yourself.'

June went ahead; and did not enjoy herself.

It was a blessed relief to be released at last and sent out on the beat again, in the fresh air on a crisp, sunny afternoon. Viv Martella was still in the station, methodically and miserably doing a body search on two of the other women. One of the men had begun demanding his solicitor, had emptied his pockets of some useless bits and pieces, and then gone pale and thrown up all over the floor. Out here the sun was shining, the occasional bird sang – on the edge of a cemetery or above one of the dusty little council gardens with their vandalized benches – and the bells were ringing.

Bells were ringing. June found herself drawn across the street to the railings of a church. It made a pretty picture, a load of sentimental nonsense, up the path to the church door. The bride in white, giggling and bumping suggestively into the laughing groom beside her, had a cheap little face and a cheap layer of lipstick on her mouth; but she was happy, and the friends throwing rice and confetti and some other unmentionable fragments were laughing and enjoying it all. It was sweet and silly. June felt a tug of envy. Without making it too obvious, she peered through the railings as the photographer positioned himself and began waving orders, directing bride and groom and the bridesmaids and the parents this way and that.

They were all having a marvellous time.

And then she got a good look at the bridegroom's face as he leered and postured for the benefit of the photographer.

She moved her PR close to her mouth. 'Sierra Oscar. Sierra Oscar from six-four-three. Receiving? Over.'

'Go ahead, June.' It was Viv Martella, back at the switchboard and sounding cheerful about it.

'Is Taffy around?'

'I think so. Hang on. Taff!' The shout nearly scorched June Ackland's eardrums. 'What's up?' Viv was asking. 'You found the other pig?'

Pig? She had forgotten the dramas of the early morning. 'Better than that,' she said.

Taffy Edwards came through. 'Hello, June.'

'What was the name of that bloke you were supposed to be in court with last week? You know, the firearms charge, the one who didn't show?'

'Er . . . hold it. Ricky Vassalo. Yes, that was it. Another wasted morning, that was. Why?'

June said blithely: 'I think I've found him.'

It was a pity, really. A dirty shame when they were all so pleased with themselves, and the bridegroom was so greedy for what came after, and the bride showed every sign of being in the mood once she had got rid of all the white trimmings. But the hunter's instinct overruled every other feeling. June was watching the family and the guests shuffling and nudging all over the church path, somehow unwilling to leave the solid old building and solid gravestones for the inevitable boozing and dirty jokes, when the panda car slid to a stop behind her.

Taffy Edwards was at her elbow. 'Oh, that's him all right, girl. Good for you.'

The two of them walked up the path towards the milling throng. Ricky Vassalo had one arm around his bride, another was reaching out for a girl who kept pouting at him and wiping her eyes with drunken insincerity. His father kept coming back and punching him on the shoulder, while the best man rubbed closer to the bride.

'Everyone say "suspended sentence"!' cried Mr Vassalo senior. They all howled uncontrollably. Heaven knows what it would be like at the reception – or would have been, if Edwards and WPC Ackland had not marched up the path and made their intentions clear.

Ricky was the first to see them. His boisterous swagger crumpled around him like a rainproof overcoat which had proved to be non-rainproof.

'Oh, shit.'

'Ricky!' said his bride with a reproving pout.

What had been planned as a procession of cars to the wedding reception became a procession to the police station. Trisha refused to abandon her new husband and was helped into the van beside him, ducking her head to avoid any disturbance to her blonde curls, and still clutching her bouquet as a talisman. Her father and mother insisted on coming along as well, in the best man's car. It couldn't take more than five minutes, the father kept reassuring them: it was just a formality, just a matter of charging Ricky and then they could all buzz along to the reception. Relations and friends, not wanting to miss out on anything, decided Ricky needed their moral support and joined the convoy. Some of them, fortified by drinks before the ceremony and inspired by music in the church, began to sing as they drove along. The singing stopped only at the station, overwhelmed by competition from the cell block. The animal rights protesters were hoarse by now, but unwilling to give up.

'I'm glad we didn't book that lot for the party,' said Ricky perkily.

He looked less perky when he faced Sergeant Cryer in the charge room and was ordered to empty his pockets. A bunch of keys clattered on to the table, followed by a tie, some shreds of confetti, a betting slip and a packet of contraceptives – unopened. Resentfully he added his gold watch and a ring.

'Right,' said Cryer. 'Richard Stephen Vassalo, you are charged that on a warrant granted at Thames Magistrates Court you did fail to appear on the thirteenth of May 1986. Do you wish to say anything?'

'Look, Mr Cryer, you know me, we don't have to go through all this – '

'Edwards, take him along.'

They emerged to a babble of gossip and complaint. Only Mrs Vassalo tried to get round Cryer and pretend it was all a nonsense, they were all having fun really. 'Bit of wedding cake, Mr Cryer?' She held out a slice from the cake which somebody was busy tearing apart with his hands in a corner of the corridor.

'Yeah, go on,' boomed her husband. 'Eat the evidence!'

'Come on, now.' Cryer planted himself in the middle of the

heaving throng. 'I'm afraid you'll have to leave.'

'Oh, no, not when – '

'Did anybody bring a bottle?'

'I've asked you politely,' shouted Cryer. 'Now push off.'

Trisha pushed aside the exploring hand of the best man. 'But what about my Ricky?'

'You'll get him back tomorrow, if the magistrate says so.'

'But it's . . . it's our wedding night.'

The best man leered. 'You leave that to me, love.'

As if provoked by the transfer of police attention to other matters, the protesters began to chant even more loudly. Ricky, being led away by Taffy Edwards, said: 'Who's making all that bleeding row, anyway?'

'Animal rights campaigners.'

'Oh, nutters.'

'They don't believe in shedding blood. You tell them you're a butcher,' Taffy gloated, 'and they'll tear you limb from limb.' He opened a cell door. 'Give us your belt.'

'And supposing nobody ate meat? I'd be out of a job for a kick-off, wouldn't I? Anyway, wouldn't be healthy without meat.' He nudged Taffy hard in the ribs. 'Good for the old you-know-what an' all. Three pints of Guinness, couple of pounds of steak, and – '

'I brought you a bit of cake, Ricky.' It was Trisha, her hair beginning to get a bit shaggy and collapse over her shoulders.

He took the slab and looked at it without any apparent appetite. 'Ta. I'll sleep on it. Remind me of you.' Looking past her along the corridor, he raised his voice. 'And tell that bleeding Dennis to keep his hands off.'

When the uninvited visitors had been urged off the premises, Tom Penny and Bob Cryer took stock, glad of the breathing space. Breaches of the peace in cells three, five and six, Ricky Vassalo in four . . .

'And the illegal immigrant in two,' said Cryer.

'Oh, I'd forgotten about him.'

'Till court tomorrow.'

'Well, let's hope we don't get too busy tonight, then.

Prisoners all been fed?'

'Taffy should be starting on his rounds now.'

In confirmation of this they heard a shriek of rage. Edwards, only recently decontaminated from his pig episode, was plastered over with a sticky mess again. This time it had reached his shirt and the tops of his trousers courtesy of the dark woman, who had given her name as Cronin, refusing to admit to either Mrs or Miss. He had offered her a vegetarian course – beans on toast – which she had rejected on the grounds that she was a vegan, and would have nothing to do with toast that had butter on it. Meat, she told Taffy, was murder. And to show how she detested murder and violence, she abruptly tipped up the tray and watched the beans trickle down his front.

'I'd like to see how a bloody vegan would make out on a Welsh hillside!' stormed Edwards, on his way to the washroom for the second time in a few hours.

'All things bright and beautiful,' the protesters began to sing triumphantly, 'all creatures great and small . . .'

Bob Cryer had had enough, more than enough, for one day. He glanced gratefully at the clock and was on his way out when Shaw, at the switchboard, called out to stop him.

'Sarge – chief super wants you upstairs.'

'What, now?'

'Afraid so.'

Cryer groaned. 'All right, tell him I'm on my way up.'

Galloway could hardly restrain himself from leaning just that extra inch forward and pounding Brownlow's desk. 'Look, sir, I'm not asking for the Crown Jewels. Just three men to do four hours apiece this evening, that's all.'

'Sorry, Roy. I don't consider the seriousness of the offence warrants overtime.'

'But I'm going to lose them, sir. They'll be playing the same game on another manor in a couple of days.'

'Well, that's another manor's problem then, isn't it?' Chief Superintendent Brownlow looked pleased with this piece of reasoning.

'What d'you mean, another manor's problem? We're all trying to catch villains, aren't we?'

There was a tap at the door, and Sergeant Cryer arrived. Brownlow looked relieved. He was always happier addressing what might be called a meeting rather than discussing things man to man.

'Right, gentlemen. Now you're both here, I do want to refer you to my memo on operational overtime and make sure you understand it fully.'

'We understand it all right, sir.' Galloway did not even give Cryer time to settle in his chair. 'But I do wonder whether *you* understand – '

'I want it thoroughly understood' – Brownlow overrode him – 'that unless it's to investigate a major robbery, a rape, GBH, or a murder, foreseen overtime will not be authorized. But the message from on high is that the new cost limits will not reduce police effectiveness. And at Sun Hill I intend to see that the message gets through.'

'With respect, sir,' said Cryer with deceptive mildness, 'the message could come down from on high that shit doesn't stink, but that wouldn't make it a fact.'

'What *is* a fact, sergeant, is that we're working to a fixed budget, and I expect your co-operation in ensuring that we do live within it.'

'Yes, well, without that co-operation, sir, this place would have ground to a halt weeks ago. Look at the time. I'm supposed to be on overtime now.'

'I appreciate all that, Bob,' said Brownlow placatingly.

'Yeah, but do *they* appreciate it? We get all this bumf coming down the line – is there any bumf going up? I mean, do they know how pushed we really are here? Just lately it's all I can do to put one man out on foot patrol on the entire ground. The entire ground!'

Galloway took it up. 'We're being asked to do this job with both hands tied behind our backs. I've had two enquiries scuppered in the past twenty-four hours.'

'Please, Roy, don't give me all that crap.'

'It is not crap, sir,' said Galloway furiously. 'We have to face the fact that just because we've reduced our overtime, that doesn't mean the villains are going to reduce theirs.'

'You're being so negative, man. If there's a cheaper, more effective way of doing our job we should find it. The more we streamline, the more money we save – '

'What are we, policemen or bloody accountants?'

'The more we save,' Brownlow persisted, 'the leaner and fitter the Force becomes. And the more resources we'll have in the future to give the public the sort of service they want. We have to look to the future, Roy. Have to be imaginative.'

'So what you're saying is that we're deliberately not solving crime now in order to solve it in the year 2000!'

'Roy, you really can be very obtuse.'

'But that is what you're saying, isn't it, sir?'

'No, it's not what I'm saying at all.' The chief super was getting very rattled.

'All right, then.' Galloway had the bit between his teeth. 'Let's take this Mrs Lambert case, the wardrobe business. She's not been banged on the head, she's not been raped. The things that have been nicked are all insured. So we just don't bother, right?'

'Nobody's saying that.'

'But you've just stopped me from pursuing enquiries.'

With a heavy show of long-suffering patience Brownlow said: 'It is simply that within the overall equation, certain enquiries are seen to be more cost-effective than others. The new guidelines merely take that into account.'

'So she goes to the bottom of the pile and she stays there. We're deliberately not solving a crime in order to save a few quid.'

'We are being realistic.'

'Then I think someone ought to tell Mrs Lambert that, and all the other poor sods who think the police are here to help them.'

'We are simply being asked to look at our work and sort out our priorities. To be pragmatic, right?'

'Pragmatic?' Galloway burst out. 'What's that supposed to

mean?'

'Leave it, Roy,' said Cryer quietly.

Brownlow nodded. 'Right, Roy?'

Galloway fought down his contempt. 'Right, sir.'

'Good. Thank you. Bob . . .?'

'Right, sir.'

'Right.' Brownlow stood up dismissively. 'Thank you very much, gentlemen.'

Galloway stormed down the stairs, not waiting for as much as a curse with Bob Cryer. At the foot of the flight Henry Talbot stood to one side, waiting to go up.

'How many prats in "pragmatic", Henry?'

'What?'

'Don't bother.' Galloway stamped past. 'I'll look it up myself.' He went on a few paces then, his temper almost spent, waited for Cryer to catch him up. 'What about murder?' he said in a seething undertone. 'What's the cost limits on that going to be, eh? Must have worked it out by now. Five grand . . . ten? What's the price of a life in this new brilliant cost-effective police force, eh?'

Bob Cryer found it wiser not to attempt an answer.

Seven

This was the worst. Deliberate violence was bad but it tended to happen on a small, calculated scale. Random death and injury like this was somehow more sickening. You picked your way through the carnage and wanted to throw up, but it was your job to put on a brave face. Some of the other faces were crumpled in shock. Others were pulped into what you could hardly call faces any more.

The driver of a Porsche belting along the road through the estate had been having a burn-up with a motorcycle. 'You'd have thought he was on the home straight at Brand's Hatch,' said a witness. Too late he had found that he had to pull out sharply to overtake a coach. The coach, full of residents from an old folks' home on a day's outing to Southend, had stopped to let a lorry out of a side turning. The Porsche failed to stop. Now the coach was on its side, the lorry was slanted across the splintered pavement in a tangled embrace with the Porsche; and a red Cortina was crushed against the overturned coach.

Sergeant Cryer and two of his men were tenderly easing dazed old men and women out through a shattered window and over the body of the coach, supporting them as they slid to the ground. There were others who would never move again.

'It's a bloody battlefield.'

Two ambulances homed in on the disaster. A doctor hurried into the heart of it. Sirens proclaimed the approach of the fire brigade. Lifting gear and cutting gear were organized with impersonal skill. It was better to treat it as a skilful exercise than to feel any personal involvement with some of the things that were staining the highway.

A couple of inquisitive boys scuttled across the road for a

better look, kicking slivers of broken glass and a torn scarf out of the way.

'Get out of here!' Yorkie Smith showed every sign of murdering them if they came within range. Then he turned his attention back to the girl in the Cortina.

Blood was smeared down the inside of the driver's door, and the man's neck was twisted at an unnatural angle. WPC Ackland steadied the girl's head, not letting her look to either side, as the firemen began to cut their way through the buckled doorframe and the weight of bonnet and dashboard which had pushed inwards and down across her knees. She was a nice girl with a nice brave smile, trying not to wince or weep. She had been a pretty girl. It would be a long time before she was pretty again. One spinning wheel of the overturned coach must have raced briefly against the windscreen, mashing fragments of it into her face.

'Keep it coming there. Keep winching. Come on.' The fire chief waved a slow rhythm, and the Porsche was lifted gratingly out of the tangle.

The man working away at the Cortina looked in at the girl. 'Just keep nice and still.' June Ackland, half sprawled across the back seat, kept her hands gently but firmly in place. The doctor edged in beside her. They exchanged glances. She could see from his expression what the score was. Here and now the damage to neck and spine could not be accurately assessed, but the betting wasn't good; and glancing down at an angle, she wondered whose job it would be to tell the girl that she was unlikely to be able to use her left leg ever again.

'What's the time, please?' the girl whispered.

'Just after nine.'

She tried to look sideways at her companion in the driving seat, but June did not slacken her grip.

'I always have a cup of tea on his desk when he comes in for nine.'

'Who's that – your boss?'

The girl tried to nod, caught her breath, and went rigid. Then she managed: 'Lester, is *he* all right?'

'He's fine.' June wondered at the unwavering certainty in her own voice. 'Just a few cuts and bruises,' she lied. 'Now, do try and keep still. You're nearly out now.'

The driver's door was freed. He was lifted out, while June made sure that the girl did not turn her head to look.

Lester brought up the total of dead to six. So far.

Some of the older people, fussing more over handbags and holdalls than the shock they had suffered, were walking back the few hundred yards to their home. There was bound to be a cup of tea there. Some of them had gone through the Blitz, and there had always, in the end, been a cup of tea somewhere.

Cryer made a quick recce of the immediate neighbourhood. The injured were being driven away in the ambulances. A school round the corner would have to be used as a temporary mortuary.

Chief Superintendent Brownlow arrived on the scene and at once had to make objections. 'A school, Bob? Surely that's not on?'

'It's half term, there's no kids about.'

'I still don't think it's a good idea.'

Of course you could expect the chief super to cover his flanks in case of later complaints. Cryer said doggedly: 'It's the only place available.'

They watched as another corpse covered by a blanket was carried past. It shut Brownlow up for a bleak moment. But then he was summoned to the school itself, to brave the displeasure of the deputy headmistress. She made it clear that in her view it was against official policy to allow school premises to be used in this way. Once such a precedent had been set, there was no telling where it might lead. Her attitude was so hostile that the chief super instinctively aligned himself with Sergeant Cryer and decided that the school had to be commandeered. He did not put it as bluntly as that – his public relations bit was, Cryer had to admit, very smooth and practised – but it was clear that he was going to get his way. So long, she implied, as they did not leave any unpleasant souvenirs behind or expect any of the school staff to come in and help.

'It's only a temporary measure,' Brownlow assured her, oozing charm and respect. 'Only until we can find suitable mortuary space.'

'Very well.' But she was still unwilling to back away entirely. 'If I should want to get in touch with you . . .?'

'I shall be here. I intend to remain on the premises and conduct the identification myself.'

'At least the headmaster will be relieved to hear that.'

When she had gone, Brownlow turned to Cryer. 'What's the situation on the driver of that Porsche? Is he going to be fit to make a statement, d'you suppose?'

'Came out of it better than a lot of them,' said Cryer grimly. 'Broken arm and collarbone, I'd say. Maybe a few other damages they'll find in hospital.'

'Was he able to talk?'

'Couldn't stop him. Quite hysterical he was. Name's Proctor. Kept saying he couldn't make sense of it, he's only had the car about four weeks and the brakes failed.'

'On a motor like that?'

'Doesn't sound too likely,' Cryer conceded.

He went back to the scene of carnage. The firemen were making it a lot tidier. The coach had been humped over on to its wheels again, and the lorry was parked almost conventionally at the kerb, though the shape of its cab was now far from conventional. The Porsche was set well apart, like a delinquent ashamed to mix with his victims. Sergeant Johnson, stooping in his bright yellow coat over the vehicle, straightened up as Cryer joined him.

'Driver wasn't kidding,' he said starkly.

'Eh? You don't mean – '

'Brakes have gone all right.'

'On a motor like this?' Cryer echoed the chief super's scepticism.

'Someone's been messing about with it. And it's not only the brakes. If I were you I'd get it on a low loader. Get it down the nick and call in the stolen car squad.'

'A ringer?'

'I reckon so. Registration plate obviously been changed recently. Nuts, bolts, screws, it's all new. Tell you what, Bob, I'll arrange for a C16 investigation if you like.'

'I'll buy that. And could you let Roy Galloway know as well? Our DI, you know. He hates being left out of anything like this.'

'Sarge,' Carver was calling, 'they're ready to bring her out.'

'Who?'

Then he saw the firemen lifting the final pieces away, and June Ackland beginning to slide the girl gently out of the Cortina. Another casualty to be added to the long dossier there was going to have to be on this affair.

'Someone take her head for me, please,' Ackland was pleading.

Sergeant Johnson's heavy frame humped across to the door. He was big, competent, and surprisingly tender. Jimmy Carver shuffled round beside him, and between them they lifted the girl towards the ambulance men waiting with a stretcher. She had gone ashen white by the time they laid her carefully down, all making soothing noises, willing her not to know what they already knew just by looking at her.

She forced words painfully out. 'How's Lester? Can I see him soon?'

'Let's get you sorted out first, shall we?' Cryer smiled down at her. When she had been carried away, he turned to Smith and Carver. 'Yorkie, I want you to go to the hospital and start taking statements from anyone who hasn't been seen yet. Jimmy, see if she's left anything in the Cortina, then get it carted away. And June, you come back to the nick with me.' He paused, looking long and hard at Smith. 'According to his little collection of credit cards and his driving licence, the bloke in the Cortina was a Lester Martin Simpson. When Mrs Simpson's been settled into the hospital and she's as comfy as she's likely to be, you know what you're going to have to tell her, don't you?'

'Me, sarge?'

'Yes, you, I'm afraid.'

'You mean tell her her husband's been killed?'

'Well, it's all part of the job.'

'But sarge, do I always have to be the one who gets lumbered? Remember Mrs Lubaczewska? And there was – '

'You'll be all right.'

Yorkie Smith departed, looking far from all right.

There were others to be told the same story. Muswell and Viv Martella went reluctantly on their rounds. Bloody pile-ups like the one this morning were bad enough. The aftermath was almost worse.

How do you ring a doorbell and tell a mother that her son has just been killed in a road accident?

What you do, as Martella wincingly discovered, is go in and talk too loudly, talk a load of old fanny about something else, anything else. And then you can't postpone it any longer, and it comes out. And then? Then the woman had acted as if it were a daily occurrence. She carried on polishing the table. When at last it hit her, she just sat down, still holding the cloth, and cried; and then asked Martella if she would like a cup of tea.

Muswell tried to brazen it out. What you did was come straight out with it, wallop, and make an end of it. That, at any rate, was what he said before he went gingerly into the hair-dressing salon behind the post office and asked for Mrs Lockett. Her mother had been one of the victims from the old folks' home. It was simply a matter of breaking the news and leaving her to it.

Face to face with Mrs Lockett, he cleared his throat twice. 'Um . . . er . . . could I have a word with you?'

'Yes?' The woman's hair was a neatly cropped advertisement for her profession.

'In private.'

They went through a bead curtain to a little cubicle at the end of the salon.

'What's happened?' When Muswell shifted his weight from one foot to another and still could not get round to the inevitable words, Mrs Lockett said: 'There's been an accident?'

'I'm afraid so. It's your mother.'

'She's all right?'

'She's . . . er . . . in hospital.'

Mrs Lockett was beginning to shrug off her lightweight pink coat.

'How serious is it?'

'I, er, I think . . .' Muswell very nearly choked, then blurted it out: 'Mrs Lockett, she's not at the hospital. She's dead.'

At the hospital itself, there was more bad news to be broken. Propped up in bed, with his left arm in a sling and a bandage swathing his left ear and half his forehead, Julian Proctor said aggrievedly: 'But I tell you, I only bought it a month ago.' He was a sallow man in young middle age, with the slack mouth of a spoiled child: not as young as he had been, but still anxious to present an active, macho image. If something had gone wrong, it had to be someone else's fault.

'Nevertheless,' said Ted Roach with a sort of savage relish, 'it's a ringer. Made up out of three vehicles, our expert Rigby thinks.'

'It's impossible.'

The young hospital technician in attendance at the other side of the bed, fitting up some apparatus whose purpose baffled even the observant Roach, looked as though he, too, was taking some warped satisfaction out of the saga. 'Had a mate bought a ringer once,' he contributed. 'Had no idea, went on running about in it for years.'

Roach ignored him and began spelling out the whole sad story to the Porsche's owner. Amongst other things, the letter on the vehicle identification denoting the year of the model did not match up to the year the licence plates were issued. Rigby had established not only that it had been put together out of three separate vehicles but that the putting together had been a skimped job. In normal circumstances it might have lasted a reasonable time. But it was amazing the things that came to light after a traffic accident. The stolen car boys were checking right now with the manufacturers, and from their own records. But in a long-running model like this, most of the parts were interchangeable. It was not going to be easy. Maybe it could be made a bit easier if Mr Proctor could produce documents –

receipts, a guarantee. Hadn't the seller provided him with some sort of documentation on a pricey vehicle like that?

Proctor groped awkwardly for the bedside phone and rang his wife. He nodded at Roach, eager to please. 'She's gone to find it, sergeant. I'm certain Mr Regan's number and the address are on it.'

'Not too reliable, that,' said the technician happily. 'Not worth the paper it's written on. I once had a mate – '

'Do you mind?' snarled Roach.

'I'm only trying to be helpful, that's all.'

'Just get on with what you're supposed to be doing, and let me get on with *my* job.' Roach leaned on the bed. 'How did you pay this Regan – by cash or cheque?'

'For the Porsche? Well, it was ten thousand pounds by cheque, of course.'

'How did you get involved with Regan in the first place?'

'It was an ad in the evening paper.'

'Ten thousand quid? For something out of an evening newspaper? You must be out of your brain.'

'Quick sale,' suggested the young man in the white coat. 'Owner going abroad. That's what they usually say.'

'It was a telephone number I had to ring between seven and eight. Well, I rang, and Mr Regan brought the car round to the house.' A voice crackled in Proctor's ear, and he said into the phone: 'Yes, hold it a minute.' He looked over the receiver at Roach, who fished a notebook from his pocket and hastily flipped to a blank page. '47 Lower Poole Street.'

Roach repeated the address, wrote it down, and got to his feet.

'How was I to know it was bent?' said Proctor, letting indignation take over again.

'I'll tell you one thing, sir. Whether it was bent or not, the evidence we've got on the way you were driving is going to leave you with a lot to answer for.'

That was not all that the hospital enquiries divulged that morning. Bob Cryer could well believe everything that Rigby had discovered and Roach was verifying. But he was taken unawares by Yorkie Smith's call from the hospital foyer.

'Mrs Simpson,' said Yorkie, 'isn't Mrs Simpson.'

'I don't get you. Come again.'

'The Cortina driver who got killed. Name of Simpson, you said. And so does the girl. But *her* name's Crisp. His girlfriend, sarge. And Mrs Simpson knows nothing about it.'

'You're kidding.'

'No. He picks her up on his way to work every morning. They've been having an affair for about eighteen months now. The only man who ever meant anything in her life, she says. And his wife mustn't know.'

'Oh, you do complicate things, Yorkie. Honestly you do.'

'Sarge, it's not my fault. And sarge, I'm not sure I know how to handle this one.'

And that makes two of us, thought Cryer morosely.

Eight

Lower Poole Street was not in one of the more salubrious corners of the manor, such as they were. Ted Roach had half expected to find a sleazy car repair bay there, or even a scrap-yard. He was not prepared for the address to lead him through a narrow doorway with a sign identifying a nightclub, nor for the framed photographs within – a selection of girls not so much undressed as suggesting what was available when the flimsy dresses were off. After an appreciative glance at one especially lithe contortionist, he pushed open the inner door.

A man with a smart grey tint down the middle of his hair, and grey eyes that were smart in a much greedier way, was sitting at a table riffling through bills and what looked like a healthy cluster of bank-notes.

His welcome did not say much for the hospitality rating of his club.

'Who the hell are you? A rep?'

Roach studied the room, marvelling. 'We live and learn, don't we?'

'Listen, mister. I don't know who you are. And I don't see reps until late afternoon.'

'Oh, you'll see this one.' Roach flicked out his warrant card. 'I represent the Metropolitan Police.'

The man was transformed. He got to his feet and pulled out another chair, summoning up a broad smile. 'You should have said. Why didn't you say?'

'I just did. Roach – Sergeant Roach.'

'Sit down. You care for a coffee?'

'Sure.' As the man turned and bellowed a quite unidentifiable name into the shadows at the far end of the room, Roach said: 'I didn't catch your name.'

'Harold.' The man looked on the verge of bending over Roach and patting his hand. 'Harold Kaye. Now, what do you think of the place? I could see you were impressed, the moment you came in.'

'Very nice. Who's Mr Regan?'

'Do you take sugar? I'd better fix some if you do. I daren't touch it myself. I've got such a weight problem you wouldn't believe it.'

'Regan!'

Harold Kaye waited until a girl had brought a tray with two coffee cups and a silver sugar bowl, and when she had slouched away he said amiably: 'Oh, Regan. Yes, he took one of the short-let offices above the club.'

'Complete with resident bird?'

'Certainly not. Nothing of that kind round here. No, very nice accommodation, and I'm choosy about who I let in. Really nice guy, he was. Left about a fortnight ago. He only had it a month. I've got some Yorkshire geezer in there now. I can't understand a word he says.'

'Regan,' said Roach again. 'What business was he in?'

'Imports and exports.'

'Like what?'

'Sports cars.' Kaye said it lightly enough, then got a look at Roach's face. The warning bells began to ring. 'Oh, come on, no. The guy was straight.'

'He was?'

'Look, you haven't come here to . . . oh, no. Not him. I mean, would I buy a motor off a geezer if it wasn't kosher? I mean, would I?'

'Did you?' asked Roach commiseratingly.

'Look, just you come and have a look.'

They went out of the back door into a yard enclosed by a mixed lot of fencing – some wooden palings, a length of corrugated iron, and a further stretch of barbed wire. The background did not do justice to the sleek, low-slung black body of the Ferrari parked close to the wall of the building.

'Ain't she the business?' Kaye was ecstatic. 'Or ain't she the business?'

'A crumpet puller, all right.'

Kaye bent over his treasure. A reflection of the gold chain round his neck gleamed in the bonnet. 'This is some motor, I can tell you.'

'Are you a gambling man, Mr Kaye?'

'Harold, please. And am I a gambling man? You are looking at the biggest punter of all time. Why?'

'I bet you,' said Roach, 'that somewhere out there in the great wide world there's a Ferrari the same model, the same colour, same licence plates. The problem is, who's got the straight one?'

Dismayed, Kaye touched the bonnet. Just the feel of it gave him confidence. 'A ringer? It can't be.'

'And the plates from this are from a write-off.'

'You can't be sure of that, not just off the top of your head.'

'No. But as a betting man, Mr Kaye, what odds are you offering?'

Kaye's hand fell to his side. 'Mr Regan wouldn't do that to me.'

'Let's wheel it in,' Roach suggested, 'and let Rigby put your mind at rest.'

If any mind was put at rest by Rigby, it was not Harold Kaye's. There was little doubt that the Ferrari was yet another of Mr Regan's interesting constructions. And in its present condition, there was no way the police were going to let it out on the road again. Kaye's plea that he should be allowed to continue using it until they really needed it was brushed aside. Galloway, appearing on the scene, made the facetious suggestion that Kaye could apply in court for a custody hearing, then hastily withdrew it when he saw that the benighted man was halfway to taking it seriously.

And so to the common factor in the case: Regan.

Nobody knew Regan's whereabouts, but within a very short time it became evident that a fair number of people would very much like to know. He had not merely sold a number of clients some very dicey merchandise: he had left a number of unpaid bills around – all very straightforward in the sense that the bills were unpaid in his own name and not under some alias – and had also done his bank as well, to the tune of a ten grand overdraft.

Galloway enjoyed this item of news. Now he knew that they would get help. Banks were very reluctant to be taken for a ride, especially when the ride cost them ten thousand pounds. Of course they would be even more reluctant to admit that the ride had been taken, even when the enquirer was a detective inspector. But there were ways of overcoming their diffidence. Some people on Roy Galloway's list owed him a favour. They were not exactly employed by the bank, but a few – and Dave Collins was one of the first of the few – did security work after retiring early from the Force, and knew where to delve, where to ask the right questions and quote the right numbers.

Not that the numbers were all that spotlessly right as far as the bank was concerned. In two months a hundred and fifty grand had gone through Regan's account, not to mention the ten grand overdraft. The security officer, Dave Collins, recited it all to a spellbound Galloway and Roach in the pub round the corner: an ex-DS himself, he had become so security-conscious that he would not let them meet him on his own premises or anywhere he might be recognized. Roy Galloway got a whiff of a feeling that certain heads were in jeopardy over the name of that man Regan.

'What about Regan's references when he opened his account? Did you check them?'

'Somebody else's job at the time,' said Collins thankfully.

'They'll be as moody as the name Regan. I can tell you that for nothing.'

'Yes, well, before I start divulging any further confidential information, what's your interest? Nothing for nothing, if you know what I mean.'

A stripper began to perform on a platform in the corner of the bar. Roach's eyes widened. He was not likely to contribute much to the discussion in the next few minutes.

'Ringers,' said Galloway.

'Motors?'

'Porsches, Ferraris, that kind of gear. Nothing cheap and nasty.'

'Then he's using other names besides Regan,' said Dave Collins. 'You can only play that kind of game for a short time before you get tumbled.' He hesitated for a moment, then took out a slip of paper, wrote an address on it, and pushed it across the table.

Galloway rescued it from a puddle of beer, and read the address: H. Wilshire, Turbery Crescent. He raised an enquiring eyebrow.

'Regan wrote out a cheque to that man for two hundred pounds,' said Collins. 'It's the only cheque he wrote out to anyone other than for cash.'

'You know anything about this Mr Wilshire?'

'Nothing. I should think he was trying to avoid paying VAT. The cheque went through somebody's else's account. Conveniently he put his address on the back.'

Galloway said: 'Ted?'

'I'll have a gin and tonic, thanks, guv.' Roach did not take his eyes off the stripper's moving parts.

'You won't. You'll get round to this Mr Wilshire, right now.'

A piece of pink chiffon curled in the air and drifted a few inches from Ted Roach's nose. Reluctantly he pretended not to notice, and turned to take the scrap of paper. Even more reluctantly he left the premises, inhaling one last whiff of pungent perfume and the equally pungent fumes of beer and cigarette smoke as he went.

There was a quite different smell on the premises of H. W. Wilshire, Joiner and Furniture Restorer. It was the clean tang of newly sawn wood. Trimmed lengths of planking were stacked against one wall, and on the other side of a partition there was the intermittent shriek of a saw spraying out a powder of sawdust to add to the atmosphere.

Mr Wilshire was a stooped little man, getting on in years but with all his wits about him. Wiping his hands on his leather apron as if to brush away remnants of one job before even beginning to discuss another, he had no difficulty in remembering Regan.

'He come in the door, same as you. Said he wanted a couple of sturdy wooden crates. Cash job.'

'Didn't say what he wanted them for, by any chance?'

'Second-hand motor spares to send abroad. Well, it's not my sort of work really, you know.' Wilshire looked around his workshop with a touch of hauteur. 'Making up bloody big crates. There's no skill in it, you see. Still, we've got to earn a living.'

'How big?'

'The crates?'

'Yes.'

'They were big. Gave me some measurements. I must have them somewhere in here. But big, anyway. Motor spares? Enough to build a whole motor, I'd say.'

'What about the cheque?'

'Well, he wanted to pay cash, but I charged him well over the odds. Took his breath away for the minute.' Wilshire dipped into his pocket for a pair of half-glasses, set them on his nose, and peered archly over them at Roach. He had the sceptical, calculating look of a cunning yet honest man. 'He didn't have enough readies on him, and I wasn't going to let him have the crates until I got paid. So we settled for half and half – half cash, half cheque. He wasn't too pleased about it.'

'I bet he wasn't,' said Roach. 'Listen, you didn't by any chance have to deliver them somewhere, did you?'

'No, he took them away on the back of a lorry.' Quite deliberately Wilshire kept the detective waiting, then added: 'Gary Sidgwick, Car Breakers.'

Roach almost laughed out loud. 'You sure?'

'Gary Sidgwick, Car Breakers. That was the name on the side of the lorry. I took special note of that. After all, supposing the cheque had bounced?'

Roach nodded appreciatively.

Even DI Galloway was capable of an appreciative nod when

the news was brought back to him. A bit more research, a careful recce around the car-breaking site, and then there could be an excuse to spin the place. Galloway and Roach felt that excuses would not be hard to find.

Bob Cryer and June Ackland sat in the car in the shadow of a railway arch. Occasionally the radio crackled into life, as Hollis worked diligently at shifting responsibility for anything that went wrong in the station during the absence of so many officers. The cartographic expert had arrived to complete work on the plan of the accident area. Where should he be put? Cryer offered only the most restrained suggestions. And they were still trying to locate Mrs Simpson, the widow who still didn't know she was a widow: messages had been left everywhere, but of course they would keep on trying.

Then Galloway came on the air.

'Right, all units. Mike Dashwood and Jim Ellis are in place. All suspects present and correct. So let's go in!'

The viaduct bisecting the breaker's yard was one of many abandoned routes between the dock wharves and sidings which had long ago ceased to handle any traffic. Dashwood and Ellis were patrolling it from behind its low parapets, directly above a landscape of crushed cars and discarded tyres. Some of the viaduct arches gave access from one side of the property to the other; some had been filled in to make workshops and storerooms. Entrance to the whole straggling complex was between two corrugated iron palisades, jagged at the top not from design but from the ravages of rust. Galloway and Roach went in first, bumping over a sunken relic of railway line. Cryer kept close behind and stopped a few inches from the CID car. He made a gesture for June Ackland to stay in the vehicle while he followed Galloway and Roach through an opening into the semi-darkness of what might flatter itself as being the administrative area. Some empty packing cases were lined up against one curving wall. On top of one was a collapsed domino effect of box files, none of them looking very convincing or businesslike. Damp dripped from the roof. At the far end was a wooden cabin stacked up on old timbers, with a flight of rickety steps up to it. The inside of its impractical window was grimed with cigarette smoke, blurring the light from the office within.

Galloway and Roach went up the steps. Bob Cryer stood well back, ready for anyone who made a dash for the yard.

Nobody made a dash. As Galloway pushed the office door open, Cryer heard a shout from inside. 'What's all this about? I'm the owner of this place, you don't just bust in here and – '

'Show Mr Sidgwick the warrant,' Galloway said to Roach. 'Then spin the place.'

Then Cryer heard his gasp, and a curse and a rush of words abruptly cut off. A man appeared at the top of the steps, spraying a handful of playing cards over the rail, with Galloway right behind, looking good and ready to push him down the whole flight.

He reached the bottom under his own steam. The light was bad, but not bad enough to disguise those heavy jowls and thick eyebrows. Bob Cryer stared in disbelief. This face had never been one of his favourites. With the hatchet jaw of a custom-built bruiser and an aggressive manner to match, this slob looked a natural for any GBH charge you might care to throw at him – the heaviest of some villain's heavy mob. In fact he was Detective Sergeant Burnside, mercifully from another manor, but in the habit of getting his wires crossed with Sun Hill.

'Come over here, you.' Galloway was at the foot of the steps as well, grabbing Burnside's arm and twisting him round against a baulk of timber. 'You bent bastard, what sort of payoff is it this time?'

Burnside tried to turn to face him. Galloway held him firm, threatening to push his face into the timber. 'Oh, guv'nor, you know what you've just done, don't you?'

Bob Cryer waved Muswell, standing in the entrance, to come and keep an eye on the other two men emerging warily from the office. At the same time Galloway waved the whole lot of them away, out of earshot. Cryer hustled Muswell and the two men against the far wall, but sauntered back and joined Ted Roach on the fringe of the argument. He was not going to miss this bit, whatever it might be.

Galloway dragged in a rage at Burnside's jacket. As it opened, a shirt button snapped. Inside, taped to the DS's stomach, was a microphone.

'What the – '

'That's what I'm telling you,' said Burnside. 'You've just fouled it up. You've just busted in on my job.'

'On my manor?'

'Guv'nor, there's a big ringing firm operating out of this yard. Stolen motors to the Continent. I've been on to it for months, and I was all set if you hadn't come – '

'On to it? Doing what?'

'Posing as a buyer. Getting myself well in.'

'Digging yourself well in, more like. Boozing with the boys, playing cards, waiting for whatever rakeoff – '

'Posing as a buyer,' Burnside repeated. 'As good as sewn up right this very day. Everything arranged to have a motor crated up and shipped out to my villa in Marbella.'

Galloway stared in loathing. Cryer felt much the same. But detestable as Burnside always had been, right now there was the galling probability that he was telling as much of the truth as he was capable of.

'Who are you dealing with?'

'A fellow calling himself Regan.'

Now they knew it had to be true.

'Only his name's most likely not Regan,' offered Ted Roach.

Obviously this was not news to Burnside. 'It's old man Galley's son, Mark.'

'Regan . . . Mark Galley . . . the rally driver?'

'That's how he's been financing his rallying.'

'Where is he?' demanded Galloway.

'Somewhere round the other side of those arches, putting the finishing touches on my motor. That is,' said Burnside malevolently, 'if you lot haven't frightened him off with all this commotion.'

'Bob! Ted! come on – come with me. At the double.'

As they began to run, Galloway shot a glance upwards and waved Dashwood to keep an eye on the space below the far side of the viaduct. Then he led the way through one of the arches and paused by a half-open door. From inside came the flash and flare of a welding torch.

Galloway nodded to Roach, who kicked the door fully open. 'Right, Mr Regan. Or Galley. Or whatever. We're the – '

There were three of them. One of them had a shock of almost flaxen hair, ruffled in a style much doted on by admirers of the rally driving ace and much flaunted on television to the accompaniment of spurting champagne. Another, in a loose red jacket, was bending over the panel of a car with the welding torch in his hand.

As they burst in he straightened up. All at once the flame was licking out at Galloway, blistering his cheeks, forcing him back against the door jamb. He was trapped, and the flame kept coming on.

Ted Roach threw himself forward. The scorching tongue swept round wildly for a moment, then the man threw it full at Roach and threw himself clean through the doorway. As Galloway brushed an arm across his face and stumbled away from the side of the door, the man who called himself Regan ducked and sprinted in the opposite direction from his murderous torch-bearer. Ted Roach chose to set off after the latter. Bob Cryer was knocked aside by the other, who cannoned into Abe Lyttleton and then sent June Ackland flying as she leapt out of the car. She hit the edge of a half-demolished wall, and went down.

Bob Cryer stooped over her. 'You all right, June?'

'I'll be all right.' She tried groggily to push herself up off the ground.

'Stay where you are. Lie still for a minute.'

'I'm all right,' she mumbled. 'I'll be fine.'

'Do as you're told. Lie still for a minute.'

Ted Roach pounded over rubble and a tangle of netting, hearing his quarry beginning to pant and whine. Muswell came in at an angle. Passing both of them, Abe Lyttleton pounced, missed, and scrambled up again as Muswell closed in. The man stared wildly around, snatched up a rusty spanner, and made a crazy swing with it. Muswell ducked, hit him hard, and caught the spanner as it fell. He kicked the man once, twice, bashed his head down to the ground and lifted the spanner.

'Pete, that's enough!' Abe Lyttleton hauled him bodily aside. 'Enough, man!'

They looked around for anyone else. Another man had been splayed against a wire-netting fence by Yorkie Smith. Further away, Regan was shinning up a mountain of scrap metal and tyres to the rim of the viaduct. As he swung his legs over the parapet there was a jubilant whoop from Mike Dashwood. He and Ellis converged on Regan as Galloway hauled himself up in pursuit. Jimmy Carver was on his way to join them.

Backing warily away from Dashwood and making a swift calculation of the threat from behind, Regan came to an abrupt halt.

Yawning at his feet was a wide gap in the metalling of the viaduct. It was the only way out now. But it was a long drop.

'Go on, then, ' Galloway taunted. 'Go ahead and kill yourself.'

'Yeah?'

Regan looked at them moving purposefully towards him; looked down; and jumped.

He landed on a heap of more old tyres, dumped in here out of the way. Bouncing and clawing his way over the hummock and out through the opening of the arch, he found himself beside one of the fitters' cars. As the fitter, already bewildered by the shouting and dashing about in which he had taken no part, yelled a protest, Regan slid in behind the wheel. The car spluttered, revved, and roared forward. Muswell jumped to one side just in time, and began to run after it, vainly swinging the spanner he was still clutching. Yorkie Smith tried to stand his ground, but Regan had no intention of swerving to avoid him. Yorkie left it until the last possible second, then nipped smartly back, grabbed a small trolley, and tossed it in a soaring arc. It went through the windscreen, spraying glass like a sparkling fountain.

The car stayed on course for a few feet, then went mad. It swerved at an impossible angle towards the wall, struck, tried to spin right round, and at last turned over on its side and slid along the ground in a shower of grit and more shards of glass.

'Get him out!' Muswell stooped by the driver's door and got his arm round Regan's shoulders, heaving him out.

Regan let out a yelp of agony. He tried to get up, then let himself curl up on the ground.

Ted Roach was on his knees beside him. 'Where's it hurt?'

'My leg. Christ, my leg.'

'Your leg, eh?' Roach thrust his face into Regan's. 'Six people have died because of your iffy motors. If I had my way you'd be number seven.'

His right fist was raised when Bob Cryer pushed his way in between them. 'All right, Ted, all right. Come on, the lot of you.'

Ted Roach was seething all the way back to the nick. If Cryer hadn't intervened at that moment, he would have throttled the bastard. He knew he could have done and would have done it.

But now it was all routine. Official mopping-up and filling in reports.

They were all winded, but still jubilant. In the information room Tom Penny fished out cans of beer and offered congratulations. He swore that he was sorry he had missed the fun; but then looked at a gash along Jimmy Carver's cheek, and the increasingly colourful bruise below June Ackland's left eye, and perhaps was not so sure.

'Sit down, Bob,' said Dashwood euphorically. 'Take the weight off your old legs.'

'Why not?' Cryer looked at Galloway. 'Better than having your eyebrows set alight, I suppose. Red hair's one thing, Roy. Flaming red hair's quite another, eh?'

Galloway was staring past him. Through the babble he muttered: 'That wally Burnside – he's not satisfied with creeping on to the manor and pulling strokes behind my back. Now he's trying to pull our crumpet.'

They sized up the couple by the map chest. June, propped against one corner, was thoughtfully sipping a glass of fruit juice. DS Burnside was making a big show of studying her bruise, and was reaching out to touch it when she knocked his hand aside.

'A touch of the Viking, you know,' said Dashwood. 'Rape and pillage and all that. Come to think of it, he does have a longboat moored up the river Lea.'

'What he needs,' said Cryer, 'is a longboat right up his arse.'

Burnside leaned closer to June and started to talk to her in an unusually subdued voice. Her expression did not suggest that his intimate communications were of any great interest.

'You know,' Roach was shouting, waving a can of beer until it frothed over the rim, 'I reckon after today I'm a pretty good candidate for the Robbery Squad. Best references, suitable for immediate promotion.'

'All that glamour, booze, loose women? It'd do you no good.' Cryer sighed, and put his can down. 'I don't know why we're having this piss-up. I'm in no mood for it.'

'Speak for yourself, mate.'

There was a further outburst of incoherent jokes and abusive shouts as Hollis put his head timidly round the door.

'Sergeant . . .'

'Which one?' came an answering bellow.

'Sergeant Cryer.' Hollis looked back at a woman standing close behind him. 'Sorry, sarge, but I couldn't get through from the switchboard, or anyway nobody seemed to hear me, and – '

'All right, Reg, all right.' Cryer moved past him. 'What can I do for you, madam?'

'I'm sorry to bother you, but you put a note in my letterbox.'

'Letterbox?'

'I'm Mrs Simpson.' While Cryer fumbled for words, she said apologetically: 'I went to a friend's yesterday and stayed the night. I didn't get back until – '

'I quite understand. It's all right, love. Let's go somewhere a bit quieter, shall we?'

She had a pleasant diffident smile. Her eyes were appealing – in both senses of the word. She was asking him something, a bit fearful but not yet expecting anything too terrible.

'I hope I'm not taking you away from anything. You seem to be enjoying yourself.'

Not much, thought Cryer. Not much, really.

The noise went on as he closed the door, fading into the background but still raucously there. It was one hell of a background for what he had to say. Yorkie Smith was not, after all, the one who was going to have to tell Mrs Simpson that her husband had been killed.

Nine

It was PC Abel Lyttleton's first big solo opportunity since joining the Sun Hill team. Here was a chance to star – to rise, quite literally, to dizzy heights. Unfortunately heights did make Lyttleton very dizzy. Now that it had come, he was not sure that he was up to it: not that far up.

He stood beside WPC Ackland, craning his neck and staring unhappily at the edge of the roof far above. Then, like other onlookers in the street, he dodged as two roof tiles came sailing down to smash themselves on the pavement.

One woman stood her ground. Her hair in curlers, she had come out for some urgent shopping and she intended to get it done. 'Look,' she yelled at an invisible figure on the roof, 'if you've got any more to drop, then drop 'em and be done with it. I need some bleach.'

'What's the problem?' Abe Lyttleton demanded.

'Stand over here,' advised a man cowering in the nearby pub doorway, 'or you'll be the problem.'

'Go up and get the silly sod down,' said the woman.

For once, it appeared, the general public believed that the police had their uses. But Lyttleton could not picture himself shinning up three storeys, even with the aid of a drainpipe. Nor did he even fancy finding a way up from inside. The mere thought of being out on a roof at that height turned his stomach.

'Hey, you up there!' June Ackland challenged. 'What d'you think you're doing?'

The man in the pub doorway peered out. 'He's on the Youth Opportunities Scheme, love. Creating jobs for roofing apprentices.'

Above them something moved. Lyttleton and Ackland stood

back a few paces, to see a man's head appear above the guttering. He jabbed a thumb down at the street. 'See those tiles there?'

'I see them,' said June.

'Well, they're mine. I brought 'em up here, I fixed 'em up here, and now I'm stripping 'em down again.'

A balding man a few yards away from June Ackland let out a small cheer. 'Good for you, mate. Take 'em right down to the rafters.'

'Why *is* he up there?' asked June.

'No idea. But I'm all for encouraging people.'

June and Lyttleton went on staring upwards. The man on the roof edged back up the slope a bit, quite unconcerned about the height or the smoothness of the tiles. With a cheerful flourish he lifted two more of them from their setting and tossed them out in a wide arc. They split into a dozen lumps, skidding away towards the kerb. It was no good for anyone's morale, thought Lyttleton unhappily, just to stand here and stare upwards, waiting for the next batch.

June shared his view. 'I think we should call the brigade.'

'You think he means to strip the whole roof?'

'Why should he? Anyway, we won't give him the time.'

'He can do an awful lot of damage,' said Lyttleton, 'and the situation will have been severely aggravated.'

June Ackland wrenched her gaze away from the guttering above. '"The situation will have been severely aggravated . . ."? Have you just joined the Tory Party, Abe?'

'They're too left-wing for me.'

A woman pushing a pram round the corner stopped just in time as a tile bounced down the roof, struck the head of a drainpipe at an angle, and came down edge-on a few inches before her.

'Right,' said June. 'You'd better get up there and arrest him.'

That was what Lyttleton had been telling himself from the moment the incident started; and then talking himself out of listening to himself.

'I suffer from vertigo.'

'I'm not that keen on Greek food myself,' said June heartlessly. 'Look, we have got to get up there.' As a tile struck the bumper of a stationary car, she shouted up once more. 'All right, all right. Now you've got everyone's attention, pack it in.'

'I'll stop when I get me money.'

'What money?'

'Ask that bastard inside there. I've been reasonable for months. Just you go and ask that bastard.'

An elderly woman who had been enjoying the spectacle until now was incensed by this. 'Watch your bloody language!'

June persevered. It was difficult to reason with somebody at the top of your voice, with an eager audience ready to pick on every word – and any sign of weakness. 'It's none of my business what you do to his roof, but what you're doing is a menace to the public. You're in trouble with the law. D'you get that?'

'Get me my money,' came the reply. 'Then we'll see. I give you ten minutes.'

'Ten minutes, love,' said the man in the doorway. 'Plenty of time to get the SAS down here.'

Abe Lyttleton decided to show some initiative. Without making too cowardly a dash for cover, he went to the door of the grocery shop directly below the roof demolisher, and tried to make a slow, authoritative entrance.

The owner's dark upper lip was dewy with sweat. His Pakistan accent made his protest a switchback of near-incoherence. 'What good if you stand about there, looking? He destroys my property . . . is mad . . . you let him go on with it, you do nothing . . .'

'Mr Mohammed, I get the impression that there is some question of money involved.'

'No question. No question at all.'

'He says they're his tiles.'

'Officer, it is *my* roof.'

'Nobody's disputing that, but – '

'How come they are his tiles if they are attached to my roof, eh?'

'Why is he pulling them off, then, and chucking them down?'

'He is breaking the law. You must stop him.'

In the doorway June Ackland said: 'We appear to have stopped him for a while, anyway. I still think we should call the brigade. He's only given us ten minutes.'

There was another crash out in the street.

'Correction,' said June. 'He hasn't given us ten minutes.'

As Mohammed held out his arms imploringly, Lyttleton said: 'Is there a reason why he's up there, or did he just pick you out of the phone book?'

It all fitted too predictably with what they could have pieced together from events outside, where the instigator of the trouble was reducing certain items to pieces. Mohammed had engaged the man, Brough, to provide him with a completely new roof in place of an existing one which had a nasty habit of letting in the wind and the rain. Parts of the old one had been dangerous, and tiles had fallen off from time to time – though not at the rate at which they were descending right now. The shopkeeper vowed that he had paid Brough in full. But the man was a crook. He had shown up and demanded more money. 'Money with menaces' – Mr Mohammed had picked the phrase up somewhere, and used it with great fervour. And the job was not very good anyway. 'What you call a cowboy' – another addition to his vocabulary. He was firm in his assertion that he had paid Brough in full even though the man did not deserve it. Brough, judging from a fresh series of impacts outside, took a different viewpoint.

Lyttleton and Ackland went out into the open again.

A little girl danced up and down on the far pavement. 'Go on, mister, one more!'

'Don't you start joining in.' Lyttleton shooed her away and said quietly: 'Well, we've landed ourselves in the middle of a financial dispute.'

'What's the matter with these people: don't they keep books, and receipts, and that sort of thing?'

The truth was, as they both irritably knew, that if Brough had not been throwing stuff all over the street, it would have been no concern of the police. Questions of financial contracts and standards of workmanship ought to be settled in the appropriate courts. The public highway was in no sense appropriate.

'How the hell did he get up there?' Abe Lyttleton speculated.

'By a ladder, I suppose.'

'What ladder? Where?'

'Well, I don't know. Round the back, maybe.'

'There isn't a back. I know the next street, and the way the houses are set against this lot, there's nowhere you could get a ladder in.'

'Skylight?'

'Can you see one?'

They backed away as far as they could to get a better view. The move was misinterpreted. The little girl, keeping her distance but not missing anything, jeered: 'They ain't going to do nothing. Hey, mister – they're not going to do a thing.'

'Do you want to get arrested?' June snapped.

'Me? What 'ave I done?'

'Inciting a riot and causing a civil disturbance. Now get lost!' She turned to Lyttleton. 'You know, we're going to have to get this road blocked off before someone gets hurt. Tell you what – you raise Sergeant Cryer and see who he can get along, and I'll go up to one of these flats on this side. Maybe I'll be able to get a better view of the scenery.'

The high-rise angle on the scenery was undoubtedly interesting, though a short distance could be an infinity when you thought of what lay so far below in the gap between one vantage point and another. June was leaning on the windowframe of a fifth-floor flat. Brough was propped unconcernedly against a chimneypiece only a few feet below her; but the void between them was unbridgeable. He saw her, and waved as if inviting her to join him.

She cried: 'Look, why don't you get down off there and talk it over, man to man? Be sensible.'

'I've been sensible for weeks. Where'd it get me?'

'What you're doing now, whatever way you look at it, isn't going to get you anywhere. The more problems you make for us, the worse it's going to be for you.'

He grinned at her and waved again. He was high on the roof and high on his own zest for revenge. 'I don't care what happens to me. But that bastard's going to get *his*. He's going to suffer, that I guarantee you.'

'I'm asking you one last time. Please go down.'

He reached between his spread-eagled legs, selected a tile, slid it free, and threw it at her almost as a love token. There was a howl of warning from that chasm between them as it went down and shattered. The answer was plain enough.

June changed tack. 'How d'you get up there, anyway?' She tried to sound admiring, a fellow professional admiring his expertise.

He smirked back. 'Helicopter.'

Basically there was such a short division between them, and if it had not been for the sickening depth of that division she might so easily have tugged her skirt straight, adjusted her cap, and walked over and wiped the smirk off his face and provoked a genuine smile. Somewhere inside him he must know that he was behaving like a spoiled kid. It was all there in his face – craggy, resentful without knowing exactly what he resented, yet with a sort of bloody-minded honesty which made June feel on his side rather than against him.

Which was all wrong.

They could have talked. Could have made a joke of it – a bad joke, but a joke. Only it was not her job to mediate: in this job, you played it according to the book.

'All right, you asked for it,' she said, leaving him sitting there while she went back to the ground floor and rejoined Abe Lyttleton. At least she had one bit of news in line with what she had gone up there for.

There was a skylight above the shop, masked by a neighbouring chimney-stack. Only there might be a certain overlap of premises, and it could just be that the skylight belonged to the shop next door. They asked Mr Mohammed. He knew nothing about the shop next door, and wanted to know nothing, and if they were assisting a trespasser on his roof and infringing his rights, was that not a simple matter for the police? Forbearing to tell him that it was no such thing, Lyttleton and Ackland hugged the wall along the shop fronts and went in through the next door.

An olive-skinned man standing behind the grille of a sub-post-office counter at once lifted the flap and came out into the shop. Many of its goods seemed to be in direct competition with those of Mr Mohammed.

'Mr . . .?'

'Patel. You have come to take my statement about this present regrettable disturbance?'

'Well, sort of. You see, from our observations it looks like the only way Brough – the man's name is Brough – '

'Yes,' said Mr Patel calmly.

'The only way he could have got up on to that roof is through your skylight.'

'Yes.'

'So we would like to go up there ourselves,' said Lyttleton, 'and have a word with him.' It was untrue. He had no wish whatsoever to go up there.

'Do you have a warrant?'

'Do we need one?'

Mr Patel smiled blandly. 'I don't know.'

'Look, sir. You're assisting the police in their line of duty. We don't have to have warrants to ask for the co-operation of the public.'

'I am not only a law-abiding man, I am also a fair man.'

'Yes, of course, it's just that – '

'I will not help you to arrest Mr Brough. Better he should strip all the tiles from the roof.'

June Ackland's eyebrows rose a fraction of an inch. 'Oh, so you know this roofer?'

'Yes.'

'How?'

'He has worked on my roof,' said Patel. 'He's done a lot of work around here, he is quite well known.'

Lyttleton was at a loss. 'But why did you let Brough go through your place and get up there? Didn't you realize it would lead to trouble?'

'I thought' – Patel was still calm, with the most tranquil smile imaginable – 'that once that unscrupulous bugger next door was desperate and that he was willing to – '

'Did Brough threaten you?'

'On the contrary, I invited him.'

'You invited him?'

June said: 'I don't want to get heavy, sir, but if you don't start co-operating you're going to be arrested for obstructing the police. And there'd be a little matter of aiding and abetting the commission of a felony.'

'On such an occasion it would be an honour.'

There was a shout from next door, and another clutch of missiles exploded on the pavement. June looked warily out. Mohammed was hopping up and down, shaking his fist upwards in impotent rage.

'Get inside!' June urged.

'Get him out of the way,' came a howl from above, 'or I'll kill him.'

'Will you go *in*!' When she was sure Mohammed had retreated, swearing and wailing to himself, she turned back to Abe Lyttleton. 'Look, vertigo or not, we've got to get up there.'

'I think you were right earlier on. Why don't we get the brigade?'

'By the time they get here, the whole roof could be in the street. Why don't you use Mr Patel's skylight, whether he likes it or not, and have a word with our friend?'

Lyttleton tried to croak a protest, but he knew that the moment had come. With a dry throat he went up the stairs pointed out by the reluctant Patel, up the three storeys to an attic where a ladder was propped against the rim of a half-open skylight. Obviously this was the ladder which Brough had used. Therefore, Abe Lyttleton silently assured himself, it must be safe. He set one foot on the lowest rung. The ladder wobbled. When he put his other foot on the higher rung and began to climb, the ladder let out a loud creak and he felt it bend under his hands.

It took a mighty effort to reach up and push the skylight fully open. Edging up another few rungs, he got his head and shoulders through the gap.

Brough, perched on the roof ridge, was engrossed in levering a further course of tiles free. When he sat back he became aware of the newcomer.

'Gawd! Sending sweeps up now! You've come up the wrong way, mate – the chimney's right behind you.'

Abe Lyttleton said: 'You are endangering human life down there.'

'Not if they keep their heads down, I'm not.'

'I am ordering you to come down.' He eased himself up another rung, and the ladder bent even more ominously, squealing against the skylight frame. 'Christ!'

'What's up?'

'This ladder's not safe.'

'You're too 'eavy,' grinned Brough. 'Just keep still, now.'

Lyttleton gulped and steadied himself. 'Stop acting like a fool and come down. Pack it in before someone gets hurt.'

'I'm not budging from here till I get paid. I'll strip the whole thing. Why should he get away with it?'

'I'm not getting involved in your financial affairs, but you're breaking the law and . . . and' – Abe clung to the lip of the frame – 'you're going to force me to take action. Then you'll have no money anyway, and you'll be up in front of a judge.'

'That's fine by me.'

Brough had a cheerful, crinkled, weatherbeaten face, and his voice was amiable enough. He was obviously used to being out in all weathers, sturdily coping with all conditions and technical problems, and working hard and fast at whatever job he was on. But he couldn't be allowed to go on with this one.

Grimly Abe Lyttleton hoisted himself out on to the roof. A grey expanse of slates stretched up to the angle where the more cheerful red tiles of the neighbouring roof began – those which Brough had not yet dealt with. Brough watched him coming, clearly welcoming the diversion.

Crouching, wavering from side to side, Lyttleton clawed his way up the slope. When he was almost in reach of the amused

Brough, he looked to one side to judge his position; looked out over the rooftops.

It was a mistake. The world tilted. The block of flats immediately opposite showed every sign of swinging over and collapsing on him. And between them was a chasm deeper than he could ever have imagined. Far, far below June Ackland waved an encouraging hand. Lyttleton went down on his knees, and felt them sliding a few inches. The slates offered no grip, no hope.

Brough's grin faded. 'Hey, careful there. Careful!'

Abe got up to his feet, feeling his knees trembling, out of control. He made a wild lurch up the slope and spread his arms wide to embrace a chimney-stack.

Brough stood up, worried. 'Don't move.' He reached out and took Lyttleton's right hand, easing him round the chimney until he could sit on the ridge. 'Take it easy, now,' The skylight looked an infinity away. There was no way of ever getting back there. But Brough, catching his glance, chuckled and said: 'Time you got back on terra firma, mate. So let's go. Nice and easy . . .'

Lyttleton forced himself to move. He longed just to slide down the slates on his bottom, helping himself along with his hands, but Brough was standing up and urging him to stand.

'Don't tread on the cracks. It's unlucky.'

They slithered down, closer to that inviting, possibly just attainable gap. At last Lyttleton sagged against the edge of the raised skylight, and began to turn, reaching with his right foot for the elusive rungs. As he half hung over the edge, Brough said: 'Where you from? Sun Hill?'

'Yes.'

'New?'

'Few weeks.'

'Well, they know all about it there.'

Lyttleton felt, incredulously, both his feet on a rung each. The ladder creaked, but that was nothing: not now, not after those last few minutes. He whispered: 'Know all about what?'

'This, o' course. I went in this morning. Told 'em I was gonna try and get up 'ere. Said they were my tiles. Told 'em straight.'

Lyttleton felt even dizzier than before. 'Told who?'

'Young copper on the desk.'

'You told him about this?'

'Sure. Nothing to hide. Not so far as I'm concerned. I've got bills, receipts, materials and hourly rate, the lot. Look, I keep proper books.'

'What did he say, this young copper on the desk?' Abe Lyttleton was getting his voice back, and a fair helping of outrage boiled up in it.

'Not much. Didn't seem interested.'

'You say you've got receipts and so on. You've given receipts to Mr Mohammed for what he paid you?'

'Yep.'

'But you think he still owes you something?'

'I don't think so. I know so. Eighteen 'undred.'

Lyttleton nodded. It was time to go down. He looked back up the slope of slates, shuddered, and said: 'Thanks.'

Brough grinned again. 'I know you lot. The whole nick would've sworn I pushed you!'

By the time he got down and out into the street, still concentrating on keeping his feet moving in the right direction and his knees from going into the shakes, a police van was drawn up across the eastern end of the street, and two hundred yards to the west a constable whose face meant nothing to Lyttleton was erecting a temporary barrier. There was no sign of June Ackland.

'Looking for your girlfriend, dearie?' An elderly woman who must recently have arrived on the scene clucked her tongue commiseratingly. 'Had to dash off. Something they said to her on that walkie-talkie thing, you know, like that thing you've got.'

Lyttleton sent out a call from his own PR. Sergeant Cryer answered, greeting him with an unsympathetic demand as to how much bloody longer he was going to take over that roofer. No, June was not there: he had heard all her news, and sent her off to join Taffy Edwards on an urgent job. 'Urgent,' Cryer repeated, implying that he wouldn't mind some sense of urgency elsewhere.

Lyttleton said: 'Look, sarge, this fellow Brough says he went into Sun Hill this morning and told someone exactly what he intended doing. Told whoever was on the desk that he was going to strip the tiles because they were his.'

'He's winding you up, Abe.'

'Don't think so, sarge. He's got books, accounts, the lot. He seems a respectable kind of bloke. You ask me, I think he's had a raw deal.'

'We are not running a small claims court, Lyttleton! Bring him in. He's causing a disturbance, isn't he?'

'But he won't come off the roof. And it's very steep. We try anything, and he'll strip it down to the rafters.'

'Talk him down. Use some of that Irish blarney of yours.'

'It's not Irish blarney, sarge.' Lyttleton ventured a retort. 'It's Hackney charisma.'

'Whatever. Just use it.'

'Sarge, he's got to be got down. He's not going to come of his own accord. Somehow we call his bluff, or we put up a show of reinforcements, and somehow – '

'All right, Abe, all right. I'll get the brigade on its way.'

Abe Lyttleton had rarely heard music so enchanting as the distant sound of the fire engine siren, blasting its way closer and closer. The temporary barrier was hastily moved aside to let the engine through. The crowd on the far side began to cheer and squash closer.

A fireman sprang from the engine alongside Lyttleton.

'Cat in a tree?'

'Man on a roof.'

'Injured, threatening suicide?'

'No. He won't come down. He's unlawfully stripping the tiles off the roof.'

The fireman surveyed the littered street and nodded in understanding. 'Right, we'll get the ladder up. How long d'you reckon it'll take?'

'Soon as you bring him down, he's under arrest.'

The fireman's nod became a shake of the head. 'I can't bring him down. Physical impossibility.'

'Why?'

'It's not my job. No fire, no danger to life. Not my job to make the arrest.'

'Well, who's going up?'

'You are, mate.'

Lyttleton watched the ladder reaching swiftly and accurately up to the roof edge. The thought of going back up to that dreadful place was too much. Nobody could ask that. There was no way he could start back up. He burst out: 'I can't stand heights.'

'We're just providing the appliance, as instructions. Even if we did go up, we've got no authority. We tell him to come down, and if he doesn't want to come then that's it. No authority, you see.'

They were all watching him. The result of walking away would be more awful than starting up those metal steps. This equipment was safer than a rickety ladder. People's lives had depended on it more than once. It would be all right. This time he would be more in command.

In an undertone he appealed, so the onlookers could not hear: 'Will one of you come up with me?'

The fireman looked at one of his colleagues. 'What d'you say, Harry?'

'I don't know. I . . . oh, all right, I'll back him up.'

'There you are, constable. Your volunteer. Your lucky day. Must be the twinkle in your eye.'

There was no twinkle in PC Lyttleton's eye as he started off up the ladder. It looked reassuringly solid, but interminable. Beyond the top there was a great wash of sky. And beyond the top rung he could fall off into nothingness.

Behind him he could just feel the tread of the supporting fireman. There was no hesitating, no way of backing down.

He reached the top, held on until the metal bit into his skin, and looked up at Brough, who appeared to be taking a short breather before resuming his bombing raids.

'Right,' said Lyttleton firmly. 'You're under arrest.'

'Come and put the cuffs on, then.' Brough was as affable as ever. 'Come on, let's see you.'

'Are you refusing to comply with my request?'

'You could take it that way, yes. I'll see every tile on this roof is smashed before I leave it. You want to arrest me, you come over here. Try it.'

Lyttleton looked at the steep intersection of slopes, and beyond them to the reeling skyline. Below him, Harry coughed meaningly.

Defeated, Lyttleton said: 'Down.'

Brough's smile seemed to hang on the air above him as he descended. Then he had to pluck up the courage to radio in to Sergeant Cryer.

Cryer was not pleased. It could hardly have been expected that he would be. 'What on earth do you think you've achieved, Abe? I mean, just what are you doing round there?'

'Sarge, I think this has to be a talking-down situation. I'm doing my best, but it's going to take time and patience.'

'Time?' squawked Cryer. 'How much more of it are you going to need, for God's sake? Get it sorted out, Abe – as quick as you can.'

Lyttleton avoided the ironic gaze of the fireman, and put on an air of authority as he marched into Mohammed's shop. Mohammed was far noisier and more abusive than Cryer. Lyttleton took the full brunt of this further outburst of anger and impatience, and then suggested that it was time Mr Mohammed reached some kind of compromise. Brough felt himself wronged. Perhaps there was something in his complaint? Perhaps it was time to think back, and think over the financial implications, and if there had been any mistakes, any unfortunate misunderstandings . . .

When the storm had subsided, Lyttleton went all over it again. And the farce began again: out into the street once more, along to Mr Patel's shop once more, up Mr Patel's stairs and the creaking ladder to the skylight again. Was he doomed to go through the motions over and over again throughout eternity?

Brough was positively joyful as Lyttleton's head reappeared through the skylight. 'Hullo. The old jack-in-the-box popping out again, eh?'

'Look,' Lyttleton pleaded, 'what he's proposing is this: he'll give you twelve hundred.'

'How?'

'Cheque.'

'Scrap paper,' said Brough contemptuously.

'What about half cash, half cheque?'

'Has he offered that?'

'I'm offering it on his behalf. You accept it, I'll see what he says.'

Brough balanced a tile on the palm of his hand and contemplated the far scenery without any of Lyttleton's queasiness. 'I want it all in cash. I've come this far, I might as well go all the way.'

'You're going to need any money you can get, friend, with the fine you're going to have to pay.'

'Oh, and while we're at it,' said Brough, 'another six hundred for putting the tiles back.'

It was working. Brough still looked resolute, but something in his tone hinted that he, too, had really had enough of this. Basically he was the kind of man who would sooner do a creative job than a destructive one. When he put the loose tile regretfully back in place, Lyttleton knew they were within sight of the end.

He made the return trip to Mohammed's shop.

'If I pay, then I pay. All right. But I want to be certain that he will also pay – the law will not let him go free after all this damage, this noise, everything.'

'He'll be charged, don't you worry,' said Lyttleton fervently.

'I must be absolutely certain that he gets the full weight of justice.'

'The full weight. Rely on it.'

Mohammed sighed. 'Very well. Thirteen hundred, and that's my final offer.'

Abe Lyttleton looked out into the street, up at the sky. Over his shoulder he said: 'Don't say "final", Mr Mohammed. It looks like rain.'

Sergeant Cryer was aware of PC Carver coming in off patrol and heading for the washroom, glancing happily at the clock as he went. Any minute now he would be off the premises.

Something occurred to Cryer. 'Jim.'

'Sarge?'

'Did some bloke come in here this morning, early – something about taking tiles off a roof?'

Jimmy Carver paused unwillingly. 'Well, a chap did come in and said he had materials on a site not paid for.'

'Materials on a . . . Didn't you ask him what he meant?'

'Well, not exactly, sarge, no.'

'So what *did* you say?'

'Well, nothing.' Carver was anxious to brush it aside and be done with it, just as he had presumably brushed it aside this morning. 'It's nothing to do with us, is it?'

'Nothing to do with us? We've spent most of the day sorting this out.'

'Well, he just came in and – '

'Why didn't you get his particulars? Why didn't you call me?'

Carver looked offended. 'I used my initiative, sarge. Didn't seem any reason to go into it. Not our cup of tea at all, as far as I could see.'

Cryer whistled thinly between his teeth. 'Well, lad, just you tell that to Abe Lyttleton next time you see him.'

Ten

It had been a depressing Sunday. Roy Galloway had felt a tightening in his chest as he picked his daughter up, and found it nearly impossible to make any sort of conversation with her on the way to the Zoo. Once they had got inside he said very brightly: 'Right, what's first, then?' And it began to drizzle. Not a deluge of rain, just a steady drizzle that drifted across your eyes and brought a damp smell out of the ground and the cages.

Julia had walked gravely beside him, accepting an ice cream when he offered one, eating lunch politely, and framing careful answers to his questions about school and her friends. Every now and then she would steal a quick, furtive glance at him as they walked along, but whenever he turned to smile or wait for whatever she might be about to say, she at once looked away again.

During the last half hour of their afternoon together he was tingling with a wretched, shameful desire to get away. And he was sure that Julia felt the same.

Only once did she come to life. As they stopped at traffic lights on the way home – her home now, no longer his – she let out a little squeak of excitement.

'What is it, love?'

She pointed to a large poster on a hoarding soaring above them. The contorted faces of four young men stared out, pugnacious and derisive. Galloway would have run the whole lot in as soon as look at them. But Julia was ecstatic.

'It's the Yellow Dogs. Daddy, they're fantastic.'

She was too young for those sort of performers. But nowadays kids seemed to be late teenagers before they had even been kids.

She went on: 'They're on up the road at the old Empire, a week on Friday.'

'You'd better stay well away.'

'My friends Sandra and Greta are going. They told me last week.'

'You'd better see what your mother says.'

'Oh, she thinks they're awful. She wouldn't let me go. And she wouldn't take me.'

'I'm sure your mum's right,' said Galloway flatly.

'Honest, daddy, they're just out of this world.'

They drew up outside the house. He knew this was wrong, but he said: 'Look, I'll have a word with mum. Maybe I can get away a week on Friday. I'll fix it.'

She looked at him in momentary adoration. 'Come in and ask her now!'

'I'd better not.' As the happiness faded from her eyes, he said: 'I'll ring her during the week. I promise.'

Julia gave him a quick peck of a kiss and slid out of the car. He watched her until she had opened the front door and was safely inside the house. One of the window curtains twitched, but he refused to spare it a glance.

The sad taste of it was still with him when he walked into Sun Hill next morning.

'So it's true?' Hollis was saying. 'Henry Talbot's really going?'

'All settled a week ago,' Sergeant Penny confirmed.

'Sarge, someone ought to have told me it was definite.'

'We all thought your ears were big enough to pick up the sound waves.'

'So if I get my application in right away – '

'You do that. Only mind you don't do your writing hand an injury. 'Morning, Roy.'

''Morning.'

Galloway was on his way towards the stairs when the boom of a draught along the passage signified that the door to the yard had opened and shut. He stopped and stared.

Bob Cryer was escorting two girls into the building. One had rumpled hair with a purple streak down the middle, though in fact the streak was beginning to stray from the middle as if she had been out in the rain all night. Her eyelashes were so heavily blackened that they obscured whatever the true colour of her eyes might be. The other girl was fair and very pale, apart from a glaring bruise high on her left cheek and an ugly scratch beside her mouth. Her cheap, skimpy, off-the-shoulder dress had been torn near the right armpit.

Galloway groaned inside. He knew real Monday morning trouble when he saw it.

'Roy.' Bob Cryer looked glad to see him and to see some chance of shifting the load. 'This young lady' – he put a sympathetic hand on the fair girl's arm, and she flinched immediately – 'is Miss Lindfield. She was assaulted by her boyfriend last night.'

'Shouldn't you be in hospital?' said Galloway.

'Silly girl, she walked out.'

'That casualty department was like Piccadilly Circus.' The dark girl had a harsh, pushy voice. 'Wait here, wait there, 'old this. Drive you up the bloody wall.'

Galloway was still looking at the victim's damaged face. 'So what are you going to do about this feller that's done this to you?'

'That's what we're here for,' her friend intervened again. 'Chris Garbett. She wants to charge him.'

'Sorry – who are you?'

'Sandra Morrison.'

Sandra. It was a common enough name nowadays. Galloway hoped his daughter's friend didn't look like this one.

'She stayed with Debbie – Miss Lindfield – at the hospital last night,' Cryer explained.

Debbie nodded, and went on nodding as if in a trance.

Galloway leaned over her. 'You realize you may have to go to court, give evidence, if we charge Garbett, don't you?'

'Of course she knows,' said Sandra Morrison.

'Oh, Pete.' Cryer waved across the office at Muswell. 'Take these girls and put them in the interview room. And stay with them until I send June along.'

As Muswell came closer, looking the girls up and down and getting an answering wriggle from Sandra, Galloway said: 'Debbie, do your parents know about this?'

'No,' said Sandra. 'She was supposed to be staying with me last night, her mum's not expecting her 'ome until this evening.'

Cryer and Galloway exchanged glances. The mother surely ought to be told. But until they had taken a statement and sorted out the truth behind it all, starting a panic and recriminations now might not be a good idea. Debbie was shivering intermittently. Better give her time to straighten herself out. As Muswell began to lead them towards the passage, Galloway said: 'I'll see you later on – right?'

When they had gone, Cryer scratched the side of his nose. 'I wonder what we're landed with?'

'To be on the safe side, don't make a move to nick her boyfriend until you've copped a statement from her. She might change her mind once it comes to putting things down on paper.'

'You're talking to an old sweat, Roy.'

'I know that, but there's something about this I don't like. The way that other one kept pushing in all the time, for starters.'

'June Ackland will sort her out.'

'Look, it might be an idea if you took the statement, Bob.'

Cryer backed away. 'Oh, no. I've got more than enough to do.'

'She might open up to you more than she would to Ackland. Women are funny creatures.'

'You should know, Roy.'

Galloway prickled with a swift comeback, but held it in check. He simply nodded in the direction of the interview room – an appeal as much as an order.

Bob Cryer sighed, and went.

The story seemed brutally straightforward: crude, cheap, and obvious. The two girls had gone with Garbett to a disco the previous evening. They had danced, had a few drinks, and then Debbie and Garbett had left. They walked round the back of the building to some waste ground and stood in the fire exit doorway. Before getting all this down in writing, together with all the more unsavoury details, Cryer wanted to know that he was not wasting police time. He leaned on the table behind which Debbie and her friend Sandra were sitting – Debbie sagging, as if her forehead might at any moment drop and hit the table, while Sandra Morrison stared contemptuously at Cryer.

He said: 'Now, you know what all this will involve. Do you want to go ahead and press charges?'

'Yeah,' said Sandra, 'she wants to go through with it.'

'Please! Debbie's got a tongue. She can answer for herself.'

'I was only telling you – '

'If you interrupt again, I want you out of this room.'

Debbie jolted awake. 'No, please, don't send her away. I want her here with me.'

The door opened and Muswell came in with a tray of tea.

'That's better.' Cryer waited until the tea had been handed out, and Muswell had set himself against the wall, studying Sandra's legs. 'Now, where were we?'

'Behind the 'all,' said Sandra. 'That's where.'

'Debbie, would you rather talk to a woman police officer?'

Debbie shook her head.

'I can easily arrange it for you. If you'd sooner tell it to – '

'We kissed and cuddled for a while,' Debbie began to speak, in a subdued monotone. 'It was . . . nice.'

Then she sank back into numbed silence.

'Go on, Debbie.' Cryer waited. 'Debbie,' he coaxed, 'I have to know. I have to satisfy myself there is enough evidence of an assault. Unless something else happened that you haven't told me yet.'

Sandra glared at Muswell. 'She ain't going to tell you with that moron standing there ready to work himself off.'

Cryer hesitated, then waved to Muswell to leave the interview room. When the door had closed, he said: 'You are not helping. With your continual interruptions, you're not helping your friend. I'm telling you for the last time – '

'Oh, but he was loving it, wasn't he, bogging at her like a dirty old man.'

'Shut up!'

Debbie said vaguely: 'He put his hand up my dress.'

'Go on, Debbie.'

'I pushed his hand away. I told him I wasn't that kind of girl.'

'Debbie, I've got to know. Now, this is important. Did he put his hand on your private parts? I have to – '

''Course he bloody did,' screeched Sandra. 'And when she pushed him away he beat 'er up and raped her. Yeah, bloody well raped 'er. That's what she's trying to tell you.'

The door opened. Half expecting Muswell back, Cryer was about to snap an order at him. Instead there were Roy Galloway and June Ackland.

'Sorry to break in, Bob,' said Galloway with unusual courtesy.

There was no need for apologies. Cryer was glad of the break.

'Debbie, I'm going to have you moved to another room,' said Galloway. 'A more comfortable one than this. Where you won't be disturbed, and where WPC Ackland here can take a more detailed statement.' Cryer wondered if Galloway had been listening at the door and had chosen that crucial moment to interrupt. 'Are you sure you're up to it?' the DS was continuing. 'I know it isn't very nice, but there are other procedures you're going to have to follow as well. I'm afraid it can't be helped. One is that you're going to have to be examined by a doctor.'

'She's already been examined by a doctor at the 'ospital.' Sandra was quick to move in again. 'Does she have to go through it all another time?'

'That will have been for a different reason,' said June quietly.

'They weren't aware of all the circumstances at the time,' Galloway added.

'And if it wasn't for me you wouldn't be aware either. Debbie wasn't going to tell anybody.'

'Are you sure you don't want your parents brought in,

Debbie? What about your father?'

'He's dead,' said Sandra.

'Debbie, I do think we should inform your mother. She's bound to find out sooner or later. I think she should be here.'

'I wouldn't want *my* mum to know, I can tell you that. It's all right, Deb, *I'm* with you. It's got nothing to do with your mother.' Sandra got up as June Ackland took Debbie's arm and turned towards the door; but Galloway was blocking her path. 'Hey, what's going on?'

'I just want to have a little chat with you, Sandra.'

'Yeah, but I mean . . .' The girl's sooty eyes tried to peer past him as Debbie and June went out of the room.

'A chat,' said Galloway. 'Right now.' As the girl tried to force her way past him, he fended her expertly off so that she collapsed on her chair again. 'Just stay there. Now you listen to me, young lady, and you listen good. That friend of yours has been through a horrific experience. One she might not get over. But while she's in this nick I'm going to do my best not to put any more pressure on her than is necessary.'

'Well, you don't think I'd want to do that, do you? Come off it – she's my best mate.'

'Then stop butting in when we're trying to create a sympathetic atmosphere.'

'I'm only trying to 'elp.'

'Then don't interfere, Sandra. You're only here because Debbie says she wants you here.'

Outside, Cryer said: 'About this examination she'll have to have – '

'I've fixed for the divisional surgeon to come in. You know, Louise Figg. I'm told she's good at rape.'

'Delighted to hear it, I'm sure.'

Then there was the real stomach-turning bit. Galloway took it on himself to phone Mrs Lindfield. He made it sound as unalarming as possible, but it was a difficult trick to pull off. Tell the woman her daughter has been assaulted, but not to worry, just to trot down to the police station and have a chat. She was safe. Safe. On the phone Mrs Lindfield herself sounded somehow impersonal. If the news came as a shock, she coped: even went so far as to say in a matter-of-fact tone that she would bring Debbie a change of clothes.

Sandra Morrison was not pleased to hear that Debbie's mum was coming to join them. But Galloway was beginning to feel that anything that was bad for Sandra Morrison must in some devious way be good for Debbie Lindfield.

A change of clothing would certainly be no bad thing. Dr Figg was on her way, and having removed Debbie's soiled clothes for forensic examination, the best June Ackland had been able to offer was a blue denim coat with all the style and charm of a workman's overalls.

'Sorry for the delay,' said Galloway. 'But if you're feeling okay, perhaps you can help WPC Ackland here. Over to you, Ackland.'

The questioning took up where it had left off.

June made a preliminary note on the open page and said: 'Well, now. We got to the actual business of his hand on you. How did you react?'

'I . . . I think I screamed.'

'And when you say you screamed – '

'Miss . . . er, I don't know your name.'

'Sorry. It's June.'

'Could I have a shower or something, please, June?'

'I'm sorry, we can't do that, no.'

'A wash in a hand-basin would do.'

'Not until the doctor's examined you. I'm sorry.'

'That's a bit off, isn't it?' Sandra Morrison was back with her friend, and back in her old form.

'The doctor,' said June to Debbie, 'has to take . . . well, you might wash away evidence. Do you understand what I'm saying?'

'I think I understand,' said Debbie faintly.

''Ow long's this bloody doctor going to be, then?'

'You do want to see a woman doctor, don't you, Debbie?' June persevered. 'That's what we've fixed. But it means we have to wait just a little while.'

'You're getting a kick out of this, aren't you?' rasped Sandra.

'Please, Sandra, no . . .'

'Knickers damp yet?'

June got to her feet. 'I've just about had enough of you. We've all had enough of you. Now get out.' She twisted the girl's arm behind her back and thrust her towards the door.

'You can't do that. She wants me 'ere!'

'I don't give a damn. I don't want you in this room another minute. Now will you *go*!'

Before she could reach for the door it opened in front of them. Galloway said: 'What's going on in here?'

'This cow is trying to throw me out.'

'Sir' – June tried to keep it level and official – 'this girl is obstructing my investigation.'

'Deb wants me here. Don't you, Deb?'

'I . . . I don't know . . . I mean . . .'

Galloway stood to one side and gripped Sandra's free arm to speed her on the way out.

'I want my mum,' Debbie began to cry.

Galloway thrust his face close to Sandra's. 'I don't know what your game is, young lady, but you're going the right way to being nicked.'

'Sir.' Muswell put his head round the end of the corridor. 'The doctor's arrived. She's in the front office.'

'Good. Right, now take this young lady to the canteen and keep her there. Don't let her wander. She's a material witness.'

Muswell looked far from reluctant to accompany the girl to the canteen, sizing her up as he went.

Galloway steered Dr Figg, a maternal-looking woman with a no-nonsense smile and a clipped, reassuring voice, towards the room where June and Debbie were waiting. Then he issued instructions for Chris Garbett to be pulled in. They had plenty of back-up for an arrest now. Before he could escape to his own office,there was another message. Mrs Lindfield was in the waiting room. Well, let them keep coming fast. The faster the better: tie up all the ends, and be done with it.

Galloway hurried off. Through the glass panel he could see a plump, fretful woman talking to PC Carver, talking on and on. Even before he pushed the door ajar and heard her voice he knew the sort of plaintive, aggrieved voice it would be.

'I do hope I've brought the right trousers. She's very fussy about things like that. Wrong colour, I think, with these other . . . oh, well, I'm bound to be in trouble anyway.'

'We're sorry about what's happened to your daughter,' Jimmy Carver was saying. 'It must have been a great shock to you.'

'I was going to bring the jeans and sweater, but then I realized the jeans were in the wash.'

'Inspector Galloway will be along just as soon as he can.'

'Why should he?' Mrs Lindfield unexpectedly changed tack. 'Debbie's just another case. Of the girl who brought it on herself. That's what you all think, isn't it?'

'No, it's not like that, Mrs Lindfield.'

'I know what the police are like.'

Galloway pushed the door open and went in. As the woman began to fuss to her feet he held out his hand. 'No, please, Mrs Lindfield. Carver, you can go now.'

'Sir.'

When they were alone together, Galloway said: 'I'm Inspector Galloway. I want you to feel that we're here to help you. And Debbie. We – '

'Please don't patronize me.' Mrs Lindfield was trying to take charge and show that she was more important than any policeman. She was the one who expected service from them, not the other way round. 'I'd like the truth,' she said, 'no matter how brutal or unsavoury.'

Very well. She had asked for it. Without dwelling on any of it too cruelly, Galloway gave her the truth. It came out with clinical exactitude.

'What if she's pregnant?' said her mother when he had finished.

'I know it's not much comfort to you, Mrs Lindfield, but I can arrange for Debbie to have a scan at the local hospital. And there are organizations, sincere people who give support to – '

'To victims!' she said with a grimace of disgust. 'I won't have her called a victim. But these organizations . . . if that man's diseased Debbie, will these nice sincere people castrate him for me? Tell me that.'

'Let's just say that he'll be punished. That I can promise you.'

She was on the verge of ranting on, and he would not have blamed her all that much. But all at once the wild flailing of helpless anger deserted her. 'I'm sorry,' she said in a defeated tone. 'Giving you a bad time. I seem to want to punish everybody. Except myself.'

'What makes you think it's your fault?' asked Galloway, alert. But it dawned on him that she was not really accusing herself, just indulging in maudlin phrases rather than sit dumb and bewildered. He said: 'This boy . . . that is . . .'

'Who raped her. It's all right, inspector. I'm getting used to the word now.'

'How long has Debbie been going out with him?'

'Debbie doesn't go out regularly, not with anyone. She hasn't ever been like that.'

'But she was with this feller last night.'

'I don't suppose she was with him to start with. Not unless she's been hiding an awful lot from me. She's never even mentioned a boyfriend, not even *mentioned* one.'

'Chris Garbett,' said Galloway casually. 'I think that's his name.'

Mrs Lindfield stared, outraged. 'Chris Garbett?'

'Do you know him?'

'Do I know him!' She was struggling to regain command and put him in his place. 'Chris Garbett's not my Debbie's boyfriend,' she said imperiously. 'Chris Garbett's that dreadful Sandra Morrison's boyfriend.'

Eleven

Sergeant Cryer had seated himself, facing Chris Garbett. Mike Dashwood leaned in a corner of the room, just far enough over to one side of the table for Garbett to have to twist his neck round uneasily whenever he wanted to check on what might be threatening him.

Chris Garbett was good-looking in a flashy, self-indulgent way. It was easy to visualize him swaggering up and down under the garish lights of a disco. He had a mass of fair hair, too rich in itself to need expensive styling, and a moody mouth which must, Cryer supposed, tempt a lot of girls. Not much taste or common sense, girls nowadays. Cryer, at any rate, was unmoved by the sulky self-admiration. It was quite something else that moved him.

'That poor girl shouldn't have to go through any more of this,' he said. 'It's not right. If you were any sort of man, Garbett, if you had any decency left, you'd plead on this.'

'There's nothing to plead. You don't catch me walking into that sort of thing.'

'Come on, give the girl a break.' When Garbett tilted his chair back, trying to preserve his aura of scornful indifference, Cryer went on: 'It's going to be a hard journey if you don't.'

'Why should I give that little prick-tease a break?' Garbett stared at the ceiling. 'Little liar.'

'A liar? Was she?'

'I'm telling you, it was nothing like the way you're making out. No way.'

'What *was* it like, then?'

'Look, you know what these birds are like when they've had a few.' He tipped the chair languidly back, shrugging, inviting them to share the wink and the nudge.

Cryer waited another long minute, then said: 'Rapists aren't the most popular people in the community, Chris. Oh, you're kidding yourself how strong you are, you'll survive, the hell with what people say. We've seen it before. Big brave show on the outside, but inside . . . ah, you won't be able to come to terms with yourself. Seen it all before, haven't we, Mike?'

Mike Dashwood leaned across Garbett's line of vision, making a great show of opening a packet of cigarettes and offering one to Cryer.

Garbett took a quick, involuntary nibble at his right thumbnail. 'Can I have one?'

'Sure.' Dashwood turned the open packet towards him.

'Look.' Garbett's hand shook as he put the cigarette to his lips and Dashwood stooped to give him a light. 'All I'm going to say is, I didn't mean to do it. I was drunk.'

'Oh, so now *you're* the one who'd had a few?'

'She led me on. That's it.'

'A scared little scrap of a girl like that? It doesn't match up. Maybe,' said Cryer, 'you've got a sexual problem, picking one like that in the first place.'

'Don't be stupid.'

'Maybe you need some help.'

Garbett flushed. He could almost have been on the verge of crying. 'You winding me up, or what? There's nothing wrong with me. I don't need any help.'

'There's nothing to be embarrassed or ashamed about,' said Cryer equably.

'Having a sense of revulsion,' contributed Dashwood.

'What are you two talking about?'

'Well, there are people who specialize in your type of problem.'

'I don't have a problem.'

'All I've got to do,' Cryer went on, 'is pick up the phone and I can have someone here within the hour.'

'To do what?'

'Talk to you.'

'A doctor?'

'Yes.'

'Who you trying to kid, for gawd's sake?' Garbett raged. 'I ain't being examined by any doctor and that's that, all right?'

Cryer nodded. 'Your prerogative, Chris. Lock him up, Mike.'

Dashwood stood at Garbett's shoulder. 'Come on.'

'Hang about, wait a minute.' He looked hopelessly from one to the other. 'I want my own doctor,' he said at last, 'or there's no deal.'

'Now we're getting somewhere. Tell you what, I'll let your own doctor be present. How's that?'

'And while you're waiting,' suggested Dashwood, 'why don't you make a statement? Get it down on paper.'

'Never put anything down on paper.'

A head came round the door. There was a call for Sergeant Cryer. The implication was that it would be best for him to take it outside.

Roy Galloway wanted to know what progress he was making. Also he had a few scraps of information on Garbett. Not much: three findings of guilt, two other convictions, all of it criminal damage. There was nothing of a sexual nature. But he had something of his own to communicate. He still had Mrs Lindfield on the premises, and for Cryer's information, Sandra Morrison was Garbett's girlfriend.

'Is that right?' Cryer marvelled.

'Hell hath no fury, know what I mean? You'd better put it to him, Bob.'

'Can't trust anyone, can you?'

'Too true. See you soon.'

Cryer went at a slow, deliberate pace back into the room and sat down. He kept Garbett waiting until he could see that hand beginning to shake again, and then said:

'Sandra Morrison.'

'Who's she?'

'Your girlfriend.'

Garbett licked his lips. 'No. I don't know what you're talking about.'

Galloway went back to Mrs Lindfield and apologized for keeping her waiting. She acknowledged this with a fretful bob of the head.

'Now then,' he said, 'tell me more about the Morrison family. They live near you?'

'Family?' Mrs Lindfield snorted. 'Is that what you call them? I blame the mother for most of this.' Evidently she had now succeeded in dismissing her own suggestion that she might herself have been in some way responsible. 'I mean, look at them. Two brothers, three sisters. All latchkey kids. They've all gone the same way.'

'Which way is that?'

'Don't play games, Mr Galloway. You know what I mean.'

He thought he could deduce it pretty well, but was not keen on floundering through too many generalizations. 'Tell me more about Sandra.'

'She's the worst. When she was fourteen, men used to pick her up in cars after school. She took them home, all hours of the morning, doing God knows what. And then sit down and write her own late note for school next day. Can you credit it?'

'Sandra and Debbie seem to be such poles apart,' said Galloway. 'That's what I find difficult to understand. They're complete opposites: what could they possibly have in common?'

Mrs Lindfield pondered this. 'Well, they've no friends, don't you see?'

'No, I'm afraid I don't.'

'Look, Debbie's very shy. She finds it hard to make friends. And Sandra – well, everybody detests Sandra, she's such an objectionable little bitch.'

'Then why,' demanded Galloway, 'did you allow the friendship?'

Mrs Lindfield's attempts at haughtiness were fading. She looked lost and unable to cope. 'I couldn't stop it. Debbie was always being left out. Lonely. So I encouraged her to go out and meet people – go to discos, do something interesting, liven herself up a bit. I never thought it would turn out like this.' She had crumpled in on herself. 'Look, Mr Galloway, my Debbie . . . she . . . it's going to take a bit of time, isn't it? That medical business . . . all the . . . well . . .'

'You can be present at the examination or have a word with the doctor, if you like.'

Now Mrs Lindfield was almost panic-stricken. She wanted no responsibility, no unpleasantness. Which was perhaps how Debbie had got to where she was now. 'I'd rather wait at home than hang about here,' she babbled. 'It wouldn't be a very good example for my daughter, eh . . . a distraught mother? Mr Galloway . . .?'

'When everything's finished,' he said, 'I'll give you a call. And I tell you what – I'll run Debbie home myself.'

Her thanks became effusive. He saw her off the premises, and turned his attention to the next stage. By now, in a vengeful mood, he had no doubt what that stage had to be.

Sandra Morrison was wheeled into his office. Muswell, who had set off with her to the canteen in gloatingly optimistic mood, now looked very glad to be rid of her. Whatever had happened between them, there were signs that the girl had got the better of him.

She was not going to get the better of Roy Galloway, though she started out with every intention of doing so. 'Don't you think I've been kept hanging about here long enough?' He stared implacably at her. She raised her voice to a shrill, piercing pitch. 'Well, say something. Don't keep bogging me like that. Don't 'appen to 'ave one of them dirty old raincoats with 'oles in the pockets, do you?'

Galloway said: 'Why didn't you tell me Chris Garbett was your boyfriend?'

'He's not.'

'Sandra, we've got him in custody.'

Her mouth twisted. 'He's lying.'

'Oh, no, he's not. He has to tell the truth, don't you understand? His future depends upon it. And so,' said Galloway viciously, 'does yours, young lady. So let's have it.'

She stared hatred. The blackness around her eyes had smudged even further, as if she had been crying and wiping the tears into the mess. But she was not the sort of girl to cry – not in front of Muswell, certainly, and not here in front of Galloway.

'I don't know what sort of rubbish he's been telling you.'

'Let's hear what *you've* got to tell us, Sandra.'

Her teeth showed momentarily between her lips. Then she closed her mouth tight. Galloway sat and waited. It took about thirty seconds before the words began to come.

'I didn't tell him to beat 'er up. To rape 'er. Did I? She's my friend.'

'Then what did happen?'

Sandra hesitated again. Galloway knew he could afford to let her take her own time now. And then it all came out.

'Debbie was always boasting about being a virgin. No man was ever going to touch 'er until she was married. That's how it all started.'

'You were jealous?'

'Me, jealous? I've got nothing to be jealous about. Just couldn't believe she was that innocent, that's all. Chris couldn't, either. She was a lying cow, he said. Anyway, while she was dancing . . .'

It was smoky in the disco and there had been plenty to drink. Debbie, probably befuddled very early on, danced with a few boys she didn't know and didn't seem to want to know again. Chris and Sandra had watched her from the bar. It was Sandra who first thought of the idea and made a kind of bet; only it wasn't really a bet, more of a dare. She challenged Chris, bet him he couldn't screw Debbie. He reckoned he was irresistible to any girl. 'He's only got to look at them,' said Sandra, half scornful and half admiring, 'and they drop their knickers.'

'I've got a few like that at this station,' said Galloway, 'except they don't go around raping young girls.'

'I didn't know he was going to do that. Not really. I swear it.'

'I'll need a bit more convincing than that.'

Sandra was totally caught up in her story now, whatever the consequences might be for her. Any shame she might have felt for her part in what had happened at that disco was washed away by memories of the way she had set things up and the way it had felt at the time. Or most of the time.

When Debbie came back to the bar, Chris had asked her to dance with him. They must have been on the floor for about half and hour, or maybe a little longer. Sandra could remember it was a long time because she had been left to buy her own vodkas and orange. That was funny, though. But it was not so funny when she recalled the way they had swayed around with their arms round each other. It was what she had meant to happen; but when it actually happened, and she was watching it and enjoying it . . . well, was she really enjoying it? It must have been one-ish when they left the hall, arms round each other. And all she had to do was wait and hear from Chris whether her dare had worked. When he came back. If he came back. She did not put that into so many words, but Galloway heard the pinching of her tone and quickening breath behind the story.

'Jealous,' he said again. 'Come on, Sandra, your boyfriend going out like that with your best mate. What if they clicked? What if it turned out to be a love job?'

'No,' she shot back at him. 'It wasn't like that.'

'It must have entered your head.'

'No!'

'Or perhaps up until that moment you though your charms were so great that in the end Chris Garbett wouldn't go through with it.'

'No,' she said again, crossing and uncrossing her knees. Muswell would perhaps have enjoyed that. Roy Galloway found the spectacle an unattractive one. 'No. There's plenty more where he came from.'

'Are there? Come on, Sandra – that was the turning point, wasn't it?'

'I don't know what you mean.'

'Spite, Sandra. First of all you want to dirty up your so-called friend Debbie. Then when it went along a bit too fast, you turned your spite from Debbie to Chris Garbett.'

'Debbie *is* my friend. And she didn't ask for all that. I could 'ave killed Chris.'

'You did incite him.'

'No.'

'And now you're after punishing him because he did exactly what you dared him to do.'

'I didn't dare him to rape her.' Now she was really in danger of crying, but from anger, not misery. 'He was going to screw her, not rape her. That's different.'

'Bit of a reckless dare on your behalf, wouldn't you say? I'm not entirely satisfied with your story, Sandra. I think you took a far more active part in this than you're letting on.'

Fear began to creep through her brash defences. 'Oh, now look. Would I have encouraged Debbie to press charges if that was true? Eh – would I?'

'You've got a twisted little mind, Sandra. And attack is the best form of defence. Up until now you've covered yourself pretty well, playing the role of the caring friend.'

'I've told you the truth.'

'Would you ever know the truth if you saw it?' Galloway raised a thumb to Ted Roach beyond the glass partition. As Ted obediently opened the door, he said: 'Get her down to the detention room until I make further enquiries.'

Now it was blind panic. 'No, you can't! I'm not going into any room. Not like that. You can't do that.' As Ted Roach reached for her she slashed out with her nails. 'Get off me . . . you, get *off* me!'

Roach held her with one hand and, with commendable style in the circumstances, waved a visitor in with the other. 'Doctor Figg.'

The doctor at least was professionally unshockable and detached, but she allowed herself the quizzical lift of an eyebrow. 'Do you always have that effect on young girls?'

Roy Galloway was not sure what effect he had on girls any longer, whatever age they might be. He had somehow not allowed himself much time to find out such things in recent years.

'What news have you got for me?' he asked. At the same time he delved into the bottom drawer of his desk and brought out a whisky bottle and two glasses.

Dr Figg offered him an appreciative smile. 'I never fail to get the finest hospitality at Sun Hill. It's my favourite nick, you know.' She lifted her glass. 'Cheers.'

'Cheers. So what are your findings?'

For some unfathomable reason she looked mildly amused. Galloway felt she had something up her sleeve. But then, medics were always like this: putting on their act, playing their professional game.

Not that detective inspectors were entirely immune from such temptations.

'Gynaecological examinations usually have their little snags in such circumstances,' said Dr Figg. 'But I have excellent forensic samples for you.'

'Good,' said Galloway, hoping to be spared the details.

'Blood,' said Dr Figg, 'saliva, semen stains, pubic hair. Swabs back and front – all good stuff, Roy.'

Galloway drowned a faint hint of nausea with a tincture of neat Scotch. 'I'll stick to being a policeman, if you don't mind.'

'But you do have a slight problem.' Her sparkle of amusement was positively glittering now. 'I'd take another swig of that, Roy, if I were you.'

'Now what? Go on – you won't shock me.'

'Won't I? Not even if I tell you that our Debbie is *virgo intacta*?'

'A virgin?' Galloway choked on his drink.

'Pure as the driven snow.'

'You must be joking.'

'I would say that the young man concerned was a young man in great haste.'

Galloway coughed and waited for the raw heat in his throat to cool off. He still found it hard to accept. But Dr Figg's knowing, tolerant smile was worth more than ten other people's loud affidavits and protestations.

'Big deal,' he muttered. 'All that, just for . . . well . . .'

'It's not unusual, Roy.'

This, he meditated, would certainly bruise Garbett's ego. And there was no doubt that Chris Garbett had an outsize ego. If nothing much else.

'A terrified girl in that situation,' said Dr Figg, 'wouldn't know what was happening. It's quite feasible, really it is.'

'I know that.' He wagged his head, still incredulous. 'But to actually believe you've been raped . . .'

'Certainly. Especially if you're a young girl with no sexual experience.'

'Hold it,' said Galloway. 'When it comes to sexual experience, what about Garbett? I mean, from what we've figured out about him – '

'Bull at a gate,' said Dr Figg bluntly.

'And Debbie has no idea?'

'That she's still a virgin? I thought I'd break the news to you first.'

Galloway raised his glass to her and drained the few drops from the bottom. 'Let's both go and tell her, shall we?'

They found Debbie Lindfield putting on a pair of shoes, lifting her feet to show them off to June Ackland.

'They're the first ones I bought myself. My mum usually buys everything for me out of the catalogue.'

'Your mum does a lot for you, doesn't she?'

Debbie nodded eagerly.

Galloway led Dr Figg in, and the two of them stood over the girl, taking it easy, trying to convey the idea that the tension was off, nobody was forcing any issues.

'You feeling all right, Debbie?'

The girl's wan face showed in a timid smile how likeable it might be.

Dr Figg said: 'Debbie, this is going to come as a surprise to you. A pleasant one, I'm sure. You have not been raped, Debbie.'

Debbie, doing up the buttons of her recently laundered blouse, looked puzzled and vaguely offended, as if someone had been doubting her word. June Ackland shot a glance at Galloway, not offended but equally puzzled.

'You are still a virgin,' said Dr Figg decisively. She turned to the other two in the room. 'Perhaps it would be better if you both left while I have a chat with Debbie.'

They silently agreed on this. Outside, June shook her head and said: 'What a turn-up for the books! I'll be believing in fairy stories next. So what about the charges, sir?'

'I've got plenty of evidence for attempted rape. As long as Debbie comes up trumps in the statement. So when the doctor's finished, it's straight up to the top of the page for you and get that statement completed. And signed. Because without it we're snookered.'

'Where's Morrison?' asked June with undisguised distaste. 'What about her?'

'I'll push for conspiracy to rape.'

'Eh? Morrison was involved?'

'You don't cotton on to the full story, then?'

'No, I don't.'

Galloway told her, more succinctly than Sandra Morrison had told it to him. June listened motionless for the first half of the story, then began nodding in dreary acquiescence; then shook her head.

'Conspiracy's a bit thin, though. You'll have a hard time proving that, sir.'

'I haven't finished questioning her yet, have I? She might plead and turn Queen's evidence.'

'Fat chance.'

He had a nasty feeling June was right. Hastily he got the whole thing on to more general speculative topics. 'What I really don't understand, even now, is how any girl can send her boyfriend out to screw another girl.'

'Oh, I don't know.' June Ackland seemed to find no difficulty in understanding. There were times when that young but oddly world-weary face of hers hinted not just at the everyday disillusionment of her job but at some personal battering which she had never confided to anyone. 'I mean, she's probably never done it for love, only to keep some randy boyfriend. What else has she got going for her?'

Galloway had to admit that this was another way of looking at it: not so wildly different from some of his own suppositions, really.

'You see,' said June, 'I reckon Morrison regrets sleeping around, though she'd never allow herself to think any such thing. She can't turn the clock back, so she does the next best thing. She sets about bringing Debbie down to her level.'

'Could be.'

There was a moment of mutual respect between them, an odd drift of agreement that became almost personal. Other theories might be valid, other things might be said in the charge room or in court or on the local streets, but they shared a knowledge based on what they had seen and heard and felt. Only it wasn't really in any way personal. It was all part of the job, part of what made the system work.

'Men'll never get the hang of women and the way they think,' said June, in what might have been consolation.

'Thank God! Anyway, as soon as you finish that last bit of statement, bring Debbie in to me, all right?'

'Right . . . sir.'

But it was not all right. The pieces had slotted in so neatly together, and the rough edges had been smoothed off so professionally, that Galloway had been sure of the outcome. From now on it was tidy routine. All coherent, all wrapped up.

Except for Debbie refusing to complete her statement and refusing to sign anything. She had been told every last little detail of what they had wormed out of Sandra; had gone pale and tried to cover her eyes with her arm, blotting out filthy truths she did not want to know about; and then had said she'd had enough. She wanted to go home. That was all she wanted to do.

'But you're not going to give evidence at all?' Galloway pleaded.

'I can't. I've got nothing to say.'

'But Debbie – '

'They were my friends,' she said drearily. 'At least, Sandra was.'

'Conspiracy. Attempted rape.' Galloway hammered it at her. 'They're serious charges, Debbie. Without your evidence I don't have a case.'

'I want to forget the whole thing.'

'I can appreciate that. What worries me is, if I throw this case out, what'll your precious friend Sandra get up to next? And Garbett – he'll think he's got a licence to go out and try it on with some other poor girl, someone not as fortunate as you've been.'

'I couldn't give evidence,' she said numbly. 'Please don't force me to.'

'Will you at least think about it?'

'I'll think about it.' She said it just to get away and be done with the whole thing, not because she really meant to give it any consideration.

Galloway walked along the passage with her, stricken by the collapse of what he had painstakingly built up. 'Having to kiss this case goodbye, it really leaves a nasty taste in my mouth,' he said. 'It really hurts me.'

They reached the door. She looked at him with the first flicker of spirit, of a real inner self, she had shown so far. 'I don't think you're the one who's been really hurt,' she said. 'Are you?' She seemed to be gaining a bleak shield of self-possession by the minute. 'All this, like the doctor said to me, it's like I've been given a fresh start. It's important to me. I don't want to spoil it.'

Galloway gave in. 'I understand.'

'I don't want to relive that nightmare. Not ever. Not in a courtroom, least of all. I just couldn't.'

'It's all right,' he assured her. 'I understand. I really do. Now come on, I'll take you home.'

'No, please. I know the way all right.'

'Debbie, I promised your mum. Debbie, please . . .'

But with a new, frightening determination she had walked out and was gone.

Galloway turned back into the station.

Bob Cryer said, 'You look as if you need cheering up, Roy. A little celebration in the offing, right?'

'Celebration? Like hell.'

'A week Friday.'

A bell rang at the back of Galloway's mind. Julia. He was going to get tickets and take Julia to that godawful concert a week on Friday.

'What's all this about a celebration?'

'Henry Talbot's leaving,' said Cryer. 'Isn't that cause for a party? And it's all on the chief super. A fond farewell to his trusty creep.'

'Not Friday evening?'

'Friday evening. Everybody summoned to attend, unless on duty doing something vital – preferably not on overtime.'

'But I've got a date. Something very special. I can't break it now. She . . .'

'Oh, it's a she, is it? Knowing the number of times you've lectured Ted Roach about time-consuming habits in that direction – '

'Shut up. It's not like that.'

Cryer looked at him and got the glimmerings of the message. 'Sorry, Roy. But whatever it is, the chief super will be expecting you to get your priorities right.'

So, thought Roy Galloway as the echoes of past defections rang discordantly in his head, would his daughter.

Twelve

It sounded suspicious. In Roy Galloway's nostrils it produced a very unpleasant smell. The story itself was plausible enough, and the victim looked convincingly dazed and roughed-up and was making just the sort of noises you would expect anyone in that situation to make. When a couple of heavies bash into your office, beat you up, tie you up and make off with a truckload of sheepskin coats, you'd be expected to raise hell when the police showed up and released you. Too late, as usual. Always on the scene after the thieves have left it.

The trouble was, Galloway had heard it all before – and from the same source.

'Elkins?' he said, when Roach reported in. 'But this is the third time this last six months.'

'They do leave themselves wide open, guv, operating from that caravan. If they invested in decent premises – '

'Crawley and Elkins Transport,' mused Galloway. 'All set for another insurance claim, eh? And how much is it this time? Any idea?'

'Eight thousand quids' worth.'

'It stinks.'

The story as told by Fred Elkins was that he had been sorting out delivery notes in the caravan jacked up in one corner of the yard where he and his partner operated their transport business. Galloway knew the yard well enough from previous occasions. A board on the fence declared that the company undertook packing, storage and freighting on a national and international scale. Their two vans and one articulated lorry hardly looked capable of surviving a rough sea crossing, and barely sustained the occasional inspection by M1 motorway police; but Elkins and Crawley managed to survive, offering a cheap service to dealers and manufacturers anxious to cut down on every possible penny. Now, not for the first time, one of those vehicles had gone missing. This time, though, there was a variation on the theme. The previous incidents had been straight thefts of vehicles, lifted off the street and found minus their loads. This one was a tie-up job. The villains had rushed into the caravan, grabbed Elkins, tied up his hands and feet and gagged him, then driven the van full of coats out of the yard.

What was strange was the phone call. After tying Elkins up and lifting the van keys, one of the men dialled 999 – went to the trouble of putting a handkerchief over the receiver and asking for the police.

Roach and Galloway shook their heads. No villain in his right mind was going to go to the trouble of making a 999 call on the spot like that. If he was worried about the victim because of the ropes maybe being too tight or something, he would get well clear and then make the call from a public phone box – most likely after the stuff was safely stashed away.

'Unless they didn't have far to go,' Roach suggested. 'A calculated risk. By why take a risk at all?'

'Just to make it look good,' said Galloway. 'Make it different from last time, just to throw us. What about Crawley – where was he while all this was going on?'

'He's got a very good alibi. His accountant. He was there for over an hour.'

'That accountant's as bent as they are.'

The description of the van and its numberplate had been circulated, but it had contrived to disappear into thin air with remarkable skill. Mark you, thought Galloway, they'd had plenty of chances to develop that skill. If it *was* the two of them. And he was sure it was. Once a van dragger, always a van dragger. And the gear was customer's gear, not theirs, all covered by insurance.

He knew in his bones that it was true, but there was no way he could come out with a direct accusation. Instead he had to listen to Elkins bemoaning their loss, and the bad effect the news would have on their trade, and the likelihood of them going flat broke.

No line of enquiry was possible until that van was found. And then most probably it would be empty.

Galloway went downstairs to ask Bob Cryer if there had been any news from Muswell or Carver or Lyttleton, hunting for the missing vehicle. There was no point in badgering Cryer. If anyone had found it, Galloway would have been told soon enough, and he knew it. But he simply could not sit still.

Cryer was not in the office. In his place, Sergeant Peters was saying: 'And what gives you the impression that nobody wants to talk to you, Hollis?'

Hollis wore his familiar aggrieved expression, caused now by mental rather than physical pain. 'It's ever since I applied for the clerk's job with the chief super. I mean, I've got the qualifications, and it's more in my line. Won't make any difference to the way I behave.'

'Don't suppose it will.'

'I tell you, it's put me off going to this retirement party tonight.'

Peters glanced past him at Galloway. 'Won't be on your own.'

'And have you heard who's coming back for it? Dave Litten, of all people. Thought we'd got shot of him.'

'Bolshie bugger,' said Peters. At least on this they were agreed.

'No one'll want to talk to *him*, if they've got any sense. But why me, sarge?'

Peters winked at Galloway. 'Jealousy, that's what it is, Hollis. Touch of the old green eye. They see you as a flyer – you know, scrambled egg all over your shoulder.'

'Scrambled egg?'

'Well, the chief super started as a clerk, you know. Stood him in good stead. Never looked back.'

'Find yourself a niche, Hollis,' Galloway contributed. 'Study for promotion, that's my advice. Let mugs like us go chasing the villains.'

Hollis looked into a shimmering, beckoning future. He began to nod slowly. 'Speaking at conferences. Mm. Attending seminars.'

'Opening fêtes.'

'I think I could carry that off.'

'Some are born to greatness,' said Peters. 'Others have it thrust upon them.'

Galloway had had enough. Nothing was going to happen for a while yet, if at all. And that passing mention of tonight's party had been an added exasperation. Only worse than that. There was something he had to do. He had been delaying, hoping there would miraculously be some way out. But Chief Superintendent Brownlow had made it quite clear what he expected of all of them; and certainly officers in a position of authority like Detective Inspector Galloway had to be in attendance.

Back in his office, he picked up the phone and dialled that unforgettable number. When Maureen answered he said: 'Look, about this concert this evening – '

'You're not going to show up after all?'

'Something's happened. I wanted to get out of it, but you know what things are.'

'Oh yes, I know. Who better?'

'Look, I know you don't like that racket any more than I do, but it means a lot to Julia.'

'Glad you're aware of that.'

'Just for once you could put up with it. Right? I'll get the tickets round to you somehow, and next week I'll make quite sure of fixing something – '

She had hung up.

He was sitting rigid when Ted Roach came in.

'Guv, I've had a thought. That Elkins and Crawley team. Why don't I go on obbo tonight and see if they move the load?'

'No.'

'But guv, they could lead me to it, we could – '

'I know what you're thinking, Ted. But you're coming to that retirement party whether you like it or not.'

'Henry Talbot is a twenty-four carat prat.'

'What's that got to do with it?'

'The man is a prat,' Roach insisted. 'I don't even *like* him, let alone – '

'He's not exactly my blood brother, either.' Galloway was sure of one thing: if he had to attend that blasted party, then everyone else around him was going to have to suffer as well. Aloud he said: 'The chief super has said everyone's got to be there. So you'll be there, Ted.'

They usually enjoyed the moment when they pushed open the door of the saloon bar and walked into the pub on the corner. This evening it was different. Elbowing their way through the crowd to the bar, neither Cryer nor Galloway was in any hurry to go upstairs to the room where the party was officially being held. Cryer ordered two pints and surveyed the rest of the crowd.

It looked as if their sentiments were shared. Jimmy Carver and June Ackland had just arrived and were making no movement towards the flight of stairs at the end of the bar. June looked quite a different person, thought Galloway abstractedly, wearing a sleek khaki raincoat and with her hair like corn in sunshine – a breath of fresh air in this polluted atmosphere.

What the hell was he thinking about?

'I don't believe it,' said Bob Cryer, spluttering over his beer. 'See who's just walked in? Well, that's me off. I'm not staying here listening to him.' He began gulping the rest of his pint down.

'What are you on about?'

Then he saw. The insufferable DS Burnside had come in, looking about the bar as if he owned the place. As soon as he spotted Cryer and Galloway he came towards them as if expecting the most wonderful welcome in the world.

'Hello, guv. How's tricks?' He waved a large, meaty hand to embrace the whole scene. 'I see we've got the uniform pushing the boat out, then.'

'There's some nice boozers out in Epping,' said Cryer. 'Don't you know any?'

Galloway had thought nothing could get much worse. But Burnside's presence could make anything worse. 'What are you doing here anyway?'

'Just come to pay my respects to old Henry, of course.'

'Old Henry?' Cryer echoed mockingly. 'And who invited you?'

'I don't have to be invited. He's an old pal from way back. Know what I mean?'

'I know what you mean. Got a sniff of the free booze, didn't you?'

Burnside turned to Galloway for support. 'I don't have to take that off him, do I, guv?'

'Never mind all that. Where is it?'

'Where's what?'

'The bottle.'

'What bottle? I don't have to bring a bottle.'

'You don't get in, then,' said Galloway smugly.

'Who says so?'

'I say so.'

Burnside tried to face him out. Galloway preserved a stony stare until Burnside caved in and turned towards the counter.

'Oi, love, give us a bottle of Scotch. Cheapest brand you've got.'

Behind his back, Galloway gave Sadie a quick scowl and a shake of the head.

'Sorry, sir,' she said briskly. 'I'm not allowed to do off-sales. There's an off-licence up the High Street, about five minutes away.'

Burnside took another suspicious glance at Galloway and Cryer, still unsure; but he got no joy from them. After a moment's uncertainty he stumped off through the door and out into the street.

Cryer panted out a bottled-up laugh. 'Ought to be ashamed of yourself, telling porkies like that.'

'Didn't I do right?' Sadie was almost as fazed as Burnside.

'With any luck,' said Galloway, 'he'll have taken the hint.'

Cryer doubted it. 'He's too thick-skinned. If I know Burnside, he'll be back with a bottle of British sherry under his arm.'

The crowd was thinning out. Carver and June Ackland had already gone upstairs, and Ted Roach was beckoning from halfway up the flight. 'You'd better get along up, guv. The chief super's asking where you are.'

'Couldn't you tell him Roy's out getting a bottle?' Cryer suggested.

Roach looked blank. He hadn't been in on the joke. 'A bottle? I tell you, we should have waylaid some of the punters coming in here tonight. It's like a distillery up there. Bottles of Scotch all over the place.'

'I should charge corkage, maybe,' said Sadie.

Galloway finished his drink and headed for the stairs. One look at Roach's reddening face, and he paused on the top step. 'Go easy on the stuff, Ted.'

'I'm all right, guv. You know me.'

'I do indeed. Don't forget you've got a promotion board coming up soon. And the chief super doesn't miss a trick, my old son. So behave yourself.'

The noise hit them as soon as Galloway pushed open the door at the top of the flight. To boost up the babble of voices there was a background of steadily thudding music from massive speakers in one corner. Behind the bar across the end of the room, June Ackland had shed her raincoat to reveal a figure-hugging brown dress with splashes of coloured flowers wreathing and glowing all over it. It was not all she revealed as she bent over a firkin of beer. When it fizzed and spluttered, defying her attempts to pour a properly controlled pint, there were plenty of men only too glad to come round and offer assistance. Bursts of laughter and shouts of encouragement bellowed across the room.

Chief Superintendent Brownlow was not joining in any laughter. He came impatiently over to Roy Galloway. The party had been his own idea but he did not seem to be in party mood.

'Roy, who are those men over there?'

Galloway warmed with secret satisfaction. It was the chief

super himself who had asked Roy to make up the numbers by inviting a representative selection of local folk. Good for community relations: that had been the implication.

'Local traders,' said Galloway.

'Look more like the Mafia to me. How did they get in here?'

'I invited them. On your orders, sir. A little local colour, I think, was the term used.'

Brownlow's beetling eyebrows descended a substantial fraction of an inch. His left shoulder jerked up and forward. It was a mannerism of his, most noticeable when he was about to get awkward.

'Look, Roy, I'm about to start the presentation. I hope for your sake they don't cause any trouble. There are other guests to be considered, you know.'

Oh, yes, Galloway knew that all right. He was not sure, though, that there was any great basic contrast between the two groups: the three local wide boys with their dark glasses and raucous laughs, and the men from Brownlow's golf club with their plump and far from quiet wives. There were brash ways of being a villain, and smooth ways of being a wheeler-dealer. The aims were roughly the same.

Viv Martella went past in a puce dress which jerked Sergeant Penny's head round. Even Brownlow spared her a briefly appreciative glance, but his gaze abruptly ceased to follow her.

'And Roy . . . you'd better keep your eyes on Roach. He's drinking far too much.'

'Yes, sir.'

As Brownlow headed for the shallow platform between the speakers, with a shrouded keyboard to one side, the door from the stairs slammed open. Burnside stood in the opening. Carver and Edwards, drinking from cans of lager on two uncomfortable chairs against the wall, grimaced as he passed them.

'Ladies and gentlemen . . .'

'Here we are, guv,' said Burnside loudly. 'I brought a bottle just like you said.' He held out something unidentifiable in a wrapping of rustling blue paper.

Chief Superintendent Brownlow glared over the heads

between them. 'May I have your attention, please.'

Burnside was thrusting the bottle at Galloway.

'It gives me great pleasure, tinged with a little sadness . . .'

Burnside tried to grip the bottle under his arm and applaud at the same time.

'Right.' Galloway whipped the bottle away and put it on a table near the door. 'Come on outside.'

'. . . that we're here today,' Brownlow went on implacably, 'to say goodbye to Harry Talbot. After twenty years of sterling service, I know we're all going to miss him very much.'

There was a ripple of laughter which pleased neither the chief super nor Henry Talbot, standing with his wife in a tight huddle on the minute platform.

'What's the problem, guv?' Burnside was muttering furiously. 'I mean, what have I done wrong?'

Galloway manhandled him through the door and out on to the landing.

'Now, what's your game, Burnside?'

'What are you talking about?'

'I want to know what you're doing on this manor, my son.'

'Nothing, guv. Honest.' Burnside spread his arms wide and nearly knocked over an elderly man with a white moustache who had arrived late and was fussing towards the door. 'I've just come to shake hands with old . . . er, Henry . . . Harry . . . that's all.'

It was a load of crap, thought Galloway. Whatever his faults, Henry Talbot had always been too straight in his own mean-minded way to mix with any copper as bent as Burnside. 'You're up to something, and I want to know what.'

Burnside let his arms fall to his side. 'Look, it's not what you think, guv. I'm not up to anything. It's just a social call, seriously.'

'Codswallop!'

'On my life.'

Galloway produced the most contemptuous sound his throat was capable of.

'You've got it all wrong, guv,' said Burnside. His heavy,

purplish lips were almost pouting. 'What it is . . . but you'll only laugh.'

'Try me.'

'Well, you know how it is . . .' But Burnside was still reluctant to take the plunge.

'Don't mess me about.'

'Well, to be honest,' said Burnside in a rush, 'I fancy June Ackland.'

Galloway nearly lost his footing on the tread of the stairs. 'You what?'

'There you go, y'see. I knew you'd take the mickey.'

'How could any bird in her right mind be interested in such an obnoxious git as you?'

The pout grew aggressive. 'Now keep it down, guv. Look, I've rung her a couple of times, but she's always given me the big E. Only I sort of thought, if I came along tonight . . . I mean, everyone's going to be in a good mood tonight, eh . . .?'

From inside came a sprinkling of applause. Galloway clung to the banister rail, beginning to shake with laughter. Burnside's face and Burnside's story – too bloody marvellous for words. It was all so absurd that it had to be true.

'Look, guv, you wouldn't tell anyone, would you?'

Galloway shook his head helplessly and lurched back into the room.

The chief superintendent was saying: 'We'd like to present you with this silver drinks tray, Henry, for all the loyalty and dedication you've shown to us at Sun Hill over the years.'

'Hope he drops it on his bloody toes.' Ted Roach's Belfast accent was all too audible.

It had not escaped Brownlow's attention. 'I might add' – he raised his voice meaningly – 'that it's not often realized what a difficult and indeed thankless task you've often had. Nor indeed what it entails.'

'Being a bloody snout!'

'Once again, Henry, we'd like to thank you for all your loyalty. We all know that without it there are times when Sun Hill police station would have ground to a halt. Have a long and very happy retirement.'

Everybody applauded vigorously, thankfully, as Talbot took the tray, and a bouquet of flowers was passed up to his wife. Somebody feebly struck up 'For he's a jolly good fellow', and with deadpan expressions Carver, Edwards and a number of others joined in.

'They'll be doing the hokey-cokey next,' said Burnside. Then he brightened up, making his way round the edge of the room until he finished up at one end of the bar.

June Ackland turned with a smile to serve him; and stopped smiling when she saw who it was. Her smile was not restored by the sudden appearance of Dave Litten. A lot of water might have flowed under a lot of Thames bridges since the day when Litten had been at Sun Hill and they had had a brief, stormy relationship, but old memories could still create a nasty jolt.

A cackling laugh from the three local traders started up the tide of noise again.

Litten stared at June, stared away. 'Well, I've done me loyalty bit. Good old Henry – I don't think! I'm glad I'm on night duty. Good excuse to get out of it soon.'

Burnside leaned across the bar towards June. 'You're not on night duty as well, are you, darling?'

She appraised him for a moment. He could not be sure whether she was laughing inside or whether it was a really inviting smile she was about to offer. 'Not tonight,' she said. 'Free and available.'

It might have been for Litten's benefit. She shot him a fleeting glance, and went to serve someone at the other end of the bar.

Burnside smacked his lips. 'Quite a tasty bird, ain't she?'

'Yeah, well, you can keep your eyes off there, skip.' Litten, too, was watching June. Something appeared to tickle his fancy. 'She's taken,' he said.

'Really?'

Burnside waited. Litten said no more, but very slowly nodded across the room. Galloway was standing with his back to them. Burnside gulped, said, 'Really?' again, and got Litten's grave nod of confirmation.

He drifted away, looking round for something to make the evening worthwhile. Chances were thin on the ground.

Others were drifting away now. Henry Talbot and his wife stood to one side of the room while a few men came over to shake their hands. Rather more dodged towards the door, not wanting to be seen anywhere near Talbot: even this late on, being friendly to him might arouse suspicions of having shared secrets with him. Carver and Edwards waited until Sergeant Cryer was off the premises, on his way back to night duty at the station. Hollis, having plucked up the courage to make a pass at Viv Martella and been slapped down for his pains, followed disconsolately into the night.

Ted Roach was still drinking and still talking, growing louder but more slurred.

Galloway took a sip from the whisky glass in his hand, coughed, and decided that if Roach was tipping back firewater of this calibre then it was high time he was stopped. He held the glass out to Mike Dashwood.

'Do me a favour. Take this over to the bar and discreetly water it down while I have a word with Ted.'

'Strong, is it?'

'If Ackland poured that, she doesn't know the meaning of the word "single".'

'D'you suppose she knows the meaning of – '

'On your way!'

Dashwood made his way through the dwindling groups of dogged drinkers, those stalwarts who would not be shifted until the last drop had been downed or a bossy voice told them categorically that it was time to go home. Viv Martella, her face almost the hue of her dress, bumped against Dashwood and peered into his face.

'What's a big, single, handsome hunk of man like you doing tonight, honey?'

Dashwood flinched. Whatever mixture of drinks she had been knocking back, it had certainly given her breath quite a punch.

'I . . . er . . . I've got a sick dog at home. Got to go home and look after it. I think it's on heat.' And not the only one, he thought.

'Thanks a lot, I'm sure.' Martella reeled on her way.

June Ackland grinned as Dashwood reached the bar.

'Here, top this up for me, will you. Water's not that expensive. Be a bit more generous with it.'

She reached for the water jug. 'Funny. I wouldn't reckon you for a Scotch drinker.'

'I'm not. It's Galloway's.'

She stooped and picked up a bottle. 'A bit of colour in the dose as well?'

'Hang on.' Dashwood put out a hand. 'Where did that come from?'

June turned the bottle round so that he could read the label. 'One of the guests brought it. There's another one down there. We haven't even opened it up yet.'

'Well, don't open it. Put it to one side.'

'Why?'

'Later.' Dashwood was turning back towards Galloway and Roach. As he reached them, Roach was grumbling vaguely on about Hollis, and what a snout he was, and what he would tell him the first time he tried acting up like Henry Talbot.

Galloway's right hand was out. 'Let's have your car keys, Ted.'

'Bloody little snout. I tell you, if he ever grasses on me the way – '

'You're your own worst enemy. Let's have your car keys. There's no way you're going to drive home tonight, Ted.'

'I'm all right, guv.' Roach swayed, and gripped Mike Dashwood's arm. 'Sober as a judge. Right, Mike?'

Dashwood said: 'Guv, I've got to have a word. Urgent.'

Ted Roach sniggered. 'What's the matter, Dashers? Something you can't handle, eh?'

Galloway said, 'Stay there, Ted. I want your car keys.'

He drew Dashwood to one side; and Dashwood explained. There had been a report two weeks ago on a theft of Scotch from a bonded warehouse on Limehouse section. All due for export.

No leads had turned up so far – until this evening. Two bottles of the stuff had turned up right here at this party. Galloway was momentarily apprehensive. It was just the sort of thing his three traders might have got up to. Brownlow would just love that.

'Couldn't have been Burnside, could it?' he said with little real hope.

'Only brought one bottle, and I don't suppose that was export quality.'

Galloway jerked his head, and the two of them went towards June Ackland. Burnside watched him with an odd expression. It did not appear that Burnside had made much headway this evening.

June confirmed that the bottles had been handed over by a guest. Not, to Galloway's relief, one of the types he had invited. Unobtrusively she indicated a man in a herring-bone jacket who was in the chief super's crowd. The chief super was still there, and they were still drinking Scotch. What was more, a couple of them had several times asked for it by name: real connoisseurs, or something.

Or something.

'Right,' said Galloway in an undertone. 'This is what you do. You keep pumping them with that Scotch. Don't let anyone else touch it. When the bottle's empty you put it to one side for me.'

'You want me to open the full bottle as well?'

'No. Put it to one side and I'll collect both bottles when the party's over.'

'Please tell me what this is all about, sir?'

'If it comes off, a rare coup,' said Galloway jubilantly. It took only a few seconds for the jubilation to fade. 'Hey – where's Roach?'

Ted Roach had taken the opportunity to leave.

He groped his way into the driver's seat and got the ignition key in at the third attempt. Bloody tired, that's what he was. And no bloody wonder, after a deadly evening like that, drinking cheap rubbish just in order to numb the pain of listening to hypocritical speeches about the worst hypocrite they had ever had at Sun Hill. And now there was the threat of a real disciple of Talbot's. If anyone could outdo Talbot in sneaking behind people's backs, it would be Hollis.

Roach roared the engine and in his head roared at Talbot and Hollis and every poxy little creep like them.

He switched the lights on. Four people crossing the road immediately ahead held their arms across their eyes in protest. Reaching for the heater, he turned the radio on full blast. A disc jockey began to rave up from under the dashboard.

Roach swung out of the side street on to the main road and headed for home. Sober as a judge. Hardly anybody about this time of night, nothing to worry about, and he couldn't anyway have spent another five minutes in that grotty room with those creeps.

He began to hum a song that bore no resemblance to the song erupting from the radio. Its steady rhythm kept him awake, kept him concentrating.

A motorcyclist almost blinded him with a dazzling single headlight. Roach swore. One wheel jarred against the kerb on a corner, and he swore again. All he wanted was to get home and get his head down and pass out.

Safest to stick to the back doubles. He knew every inch of the way. Past a half-demolished chapel, turn right by the pub – knew it like the back of his hand – and down a quiet street of Edwardian terraces with small front gardens and white palings. The beam of his headlights flickered dizzyingly along the strip of fencing.

Shadows danced across the road. And suddenly one of them was the thick black shadow of a dog, bounding towards a doorstep.

Roach swore again and spun the wheel desperately. The house fronts swung towards him at an impossible angle, and all at once the white palings were ahead of him and not to one side. He stamped on the brake. There was a cracking, splintering screech, slats of wood twisted up in the air, and the bonnet of the car tilted downwards above a tiny basement window.

He reached for the door handle and tried to heave himself out, but was trapped. Then he realized he must have fastened his seat belt instinctively as he got in. By the time he had found the release and tottered out on to the patch of grass, light was flooding on to the path from an open front door.

'What's going on here?' A tall Jamaican with piercing eyes reflecting the light came down two steps. 'Hey, is this your car, man?'

'I . . . oh, God, what . . .'

Doors were opening all along the street.

'What's this doing in my garden, man?'

Roach made a run for it, towards the far, darker end of the street.

Thirteen

Bob Cryer inhaled several gulps of fresh air – or the nearest thing to it that the space between the pub and Sun Hill police station could provide – and eased himself thankfully back into the familiar atmosphere of slightly musty central heating, unpredictable draughts and the occasional waft of wet shoes and sweaty tunics. Even when the switchboard was going berserk and somebody was doing his nut in one of the cells, it was quieter here than in the boozy uproar he had just left.

Sergeant Peters looked up from the desk. 'Blimey, you're keen! Not half past nine yet.'

'Always raring to go,' said Cryer, who in fact was raring to sit down and go through the incident book and enjoy a bit of academic assessment.

'If it's excitement you want, this is definitely not the place to be. Quiet as a graveyard so far, Bob. Nothing happened at all. Not a dickie bird. Nothing in the book since . . . let's see . . .'

His meditation was broken into by a peremptory hammering on the counter. Peters had spoken too soon. A woman with a silk scarf knotted over her head was complaining, even before he was within a yard of her, about the noise up the road, the disgrace of it – 'I can't sleep, nobody can sleep.' Peters looked politely concerned. Cryer wondered who could get stroppy about not being allowed to sleep around nine-thirty in the evening.

'From up the road,' the woman declared over and over again. 'Up the road. The noise, it's a disgrace, that's what.'

'You can pinpoint the location, madam?'

'That pub on the corner. You know, up the road – down from here.'

Bob Cryer tried to work out the mathematics of this in his mind and then it dawned on him. This member of the public was making a complaint about the volume of the celebrations at the chief super's party. He contemplated intervening; then left it to Sergeant Peters.

'And they're starting up the *other* way,' the woman went on, outraged. 'What's the neighbourhood coming to, that's what I want to know.'

'Madam?'

'House on the other side, three doors down. Starting up a party, you can tell it's going to go on and on till God knows what hour of the morning.'

Bob Cryer looked at the clock, gladly accepted the routine that, compared with what was going on elsewhere, could only be described as tranquil, and went off on the dot to the parade room.

Carver and Edwards looked as relieved as himself at having finally escaped the party. Carver tugged his tunic straight. Edwards, for once, looked quite keen and attentive. The cool night air would do them good.

Cryer went down the list. That van-load of sheepskin coats had still not been located. Every eye should be kept open for the van, or even for any unlikely bunch of strollers wearing clothes of a quality to which they were not accustomed. Then, on three beat, the occupants of 43 Rampton Gardens were on holiday until the twentieth of the month. Casual attention was all that was called for: but casual as it might be, let it be attentive. Check on possible noise round the corner below a pub which should need no naming – but report back before making an issue of it, just in case there was a mix-up with late departures from the chief super's shindig. Another rave-up: a twenty-first birthday party in Vale View Gardens, going on till one. The householders had apologized in advance for any noise, and spoken to the neighbours. All the same, make sure it didn't get out of hand.

'But don't be tempted in,' Cryer warned, 'if you're invited. You're apt to lose your helmet at those kind of dos.'

'Or something else, sarge.' Yorkie Smith rolled his eyes.

Just for that, Cryer decreed that Smith could go down to Langham Sykes, the jewellers in the High Street, and relieve the late-turn PC. There was a broken window, the burglar alarm had been triggered off, and they had to wait until the keyholder turned up. It might involve a long wait.

'Oh, and all of you – have a look at the AS on the stolen sheepskin coats.' He took a note which Shaw had just brought in from the switchboard, and skimmed over it. 'Hm. Carver, you're on eight beat, right?'

'Right, sarge.' Carver waited for the worst.

'Number 14 Graceton Avenue. They've got a car in their front garden.'

Taffy Edwards grinned. 'Why don't they have little plastic gnomes like everybody else?'

'Take a panda down there,' said Cryer, 'and take the Welsh wit with you.' He waved at the rest of them. 'All right, off you go, all of you. Get out and terrorize the population.'

They went out into the night.

Yorkie Smith found himself the butt of jovial and not so jovial remarks from neighbours who regarded the frequently jangling burglar alarm as a bad joke in itself. Couldn't he shin up and stop it? Didn't he have some marvellous new electronic device that would silence it from a distance? Was it all right if they helped themselves through the gap in the window, or were those shutters electrified? He paced up and down on sentry-go, wondering when the hell Mr Sykes, or whoever, would summon up the energy to appear on the scene.

Plenty of people had appeared on the scene confronting Carver and Edwards as they turned into Graceton Avenue. A useful battery of lights from windows and open front doors illuminated the tableau of tilted vehicle and splintered palings. Neighbours of a variety of hues from pale white to gleaming black prodded their way round the car, leaning in the driver's door, peering under the twisted bonnet and trying to force it up.

Jimmy Carver moved in. 'Excuse me. Come on, sonny . . .

excuse me, madam. Could you all move away from the car, please?'

A few of them edged a few paces towards their own houses, but no more than that. Two children stared solemnly up at the police officers, giggled suddenly, and scuttled round to the other side of the car.

'Could you go and stand on the other side of the road, please?' said Edwards authoritatively. 'Back there on the other pavement. Or back indoors. Please.' When there was a clear space around the car he spoke close to Carver's ear. 'God, you know whose car this is, don't you?'

'Officer!' A tall Jamaican stood on the pathway to the front door. 'Officer!'

'Is this your car, sir?'

'No, it's not, man.'

'Then you, sir, are . . .?'

'I'm the one who rang you. Had to dial 999 three times 'fore I could raise anybody.'

'Could I have your name, sir?'

'Name? Who needs my name? I live here, don't I? This is my house, man. Twenty years I've lived here.'

Edwards said soothingly: 'All my colleague wants to know is –'

'I'm a British citizen.' He drew himself up; a man of well over six feet. 'Ex Kingston Town policeman,' he said proudly. 'Acting – '

'Can I have your name, please, sir?'

'Samuel Winston O'Ryan.'

'Used to be a copper, did you, sir?'

'Yes, man. Acting sergeant first class.'

'Right, sir,' said Taffy Edwards, inspired. 'Let's see you get all those people out of here. It would be a big help to us. Then we'll see where we can go from here. All right?'

If it had been possible to draw himself any higher, the Jamaican would have done so. With majestic tread he advanced on his neighbours.

Edwards said again: 'You know whose car this is, don't you?'

Jimmy Carver stood back and studied it. 'It looks familiar.'

'It's DS Roach's.'

'Roach? It can't be.'

'I'm telling you. Look,' said Edwards, 'there's a public phone box round the corner. You go and phone Sergeant Cryer. He'll know what to do.' As Carver involuntarily touched his radio, Edwards said: 'Blast it all over the manor? The phone box, boyo. Do *not* transmit, right?'

He stared at the crumpled, motionless car. Roach's car all right; but where had the detective sergeant got to?

The phone box round the corner had been too close to the scene of the accident for Ted Roach's liking. He had stumbled, panting, another quarter of a mile before finding one near a badly lit bus stop. Words came out as confused as his thoughts.

'Hello, Linda. Listen.' Before she could get too far into questions as to where the hell he was, and how much longer before he got away from that perishing party and got back to bed, he pleaded: 'Don't say anything. Not now. Just listen. I'm in a little bit of trouble. I've had a bang with the car.' The squawk in the earpiece did his headache no good at all. 'No, no, I'm all right. Only had a drop over the odds at that retirement party. I can't afford to be breathalyzed at the moment, that's all.' She started to tell him exactly what she thought of him. Not for the first time. He knew it all off by heart. 'Just *listen*, will you? I'm . . . going missing for a while. Until I've sobered up. All right? So if anyone calls you don't know where I am . . . and I haven't been in touch. Got it?'

As he hung up and forced the door painfully open, he had a feeling from her parting remark that she wouldn't be in that bed much longer. Same old story. She wouldn't be the first to walk out. He knew all that part of it, too, off by heart.

Trying to stay soberly upright, he looked along the street to get his bearings. Gratitude welled up inside as he saw the tattered awning of the Italian restaurant in whose corner he had settled, out of range of Galloway and other harassments, so often for so many plates of spaghetti and glasses of Valpolicella.

He made his way to the door, tugged at his jacket; and tripped over the mat inside.

'Sergeant Roach!' The welcome was warm and genuine, without a hint of any surprise at Roach's less than suave appearance, or his momentary unsteadiness. 'What a pleasure, we did not expect – '

'Luigi, listen.'

'I know, I know.' A friendly arm encircled Roach's shoulders. 'You forgot to book your table. Don't worry, is no problem.'

'Luigi, for God's sake listen. I've got to find a place where I can kip down for a while, out of sight . . . and no questions. You know what I mean?'

Luigi squeezed his shoulder. He knew, or could guess. Not all the details, of course, but enough to make a convincing scenario. And there would be no questions.

Leaving the waiter in charge of the restaurant, he led Roach out of the back door past a row of dustbins to a square of waste ground, appropriated by locals as a parking lot. Roach sagged thankfully into the passenger seat as Luigi drove the Fiat swiftly down a sequence of dark lanes to the riverside. A couple of container lorries were drawn up between warehouses and a freighter moored at the quay. Resting on the mud in a small, shallow basin was a cluster of houseboats in various stages of preservation or disrepair.

'There,' said Luigi fondly. 'This one. You sleep it off, yes?'

Roach peered down into the gloom. He could just make out the rusty skeleton of ladder plunging sheer down the green-slimed wall. It was the steepness, not the slime, which made him want to throw up.

'I won't forget you, Luigi,' he muttered abjectly.

Luigi slapped him on the back. It was almost fatal. Roach teetered on the edge, took a deep breath, and turned slowly and carefully so that he could descend to the deck.

'You sleep it off, yes?' said Luigi.

More likely stay awake till dawn, thought Roach as he clawed gingerly down, and sort things out. If ever there was a way of sorting this little lot out.

He found the deck, found his way into the cabin, and collapsed on the damp-smelling bunk. For a few seconds it felt as if the boat was spinning in a slow, sickening whirlpool. Then he slept.

The lights had not been put out, and no chairs or tables had been moved from their original positions, but somehow the room was beginning to look sleazy, sinking into a glum twilight. Sadie had sent a barman up to help shift the empty beer barrel and provide a fresh supply of tea towels. June Ackland was reassembling some of the liqueur bottles behind the bar.

Roy Galloway, deriving increasing satisfaction from the sight of the chief super and his friends still dipping their noses into that particular brand of whisky, caught a movement across the room. The door at the head of the stairs was slightly ajar. Oddly framed in the crack was the face of Bob Cryer. Something in that face boded no good.

Chief Superintendent Brownlow was watching. Galloway sauntered towards the door as casually as possible.

Outside, he said: 'Something the matter?'

'Ted Roach.'

'Not another punch-up?'

'Unauthorized parking,' said Cryer drily.

'What was that?'

'Someone's front garden,' said Cryer. 'And he's done a runner, Roy.'

It had to be a joke. But Galloway knew it wasn't. 'Is he hurt?'

'Shouldn't think so, not the way he legged it from the scene.'

Galloway pounded his fist into his forehead. This was going to be curtains for Roach if the chief super found out. There had been troubles before, but they had ironed themselves out or been ironed out. This time would be the last.

'Any idea where he is?'

'I phoned home. His missus –'

'Missus? Come off it, Bob. You know Roach.'

'Yes,' said Cryer regretfully. 'Well, whoever she is, she said she hasn't seen him. Doesn't have a clue where he is. Sounded awfully pat to me, Roy.'

'Well, he doesn't want to be breathalyzed, does he? Preparing the ground.'

'Yes, that's what I figured. And I suppose he'll come waltzing into the nick in the morning all nice and . . .'

The door was flung open. An elderly man with white hair and a very red face, supporting or supported by a woman with equally white hair of a somewhat less natural tint, blundered out on to the narrow landing.

'Steady!' said Galloway.

The man looked straight ahead. The woman, urging him towards the stairs, treated Galloway to a lofty smile. 'A lovely party,' she said condescendingly.

'Very nice.' The man began to thump his way down, step by step.

'One of the chief super's crowd,' Galloway murmured. When the door below had also crashed shut, he asked: 'And where's the car?'

'I'm having it towed in.'

'Much damage?'

'Superficial, front end, according to Carver. I've fixed for it to be parked nose against the wall so no one can see it.'

'And the people who saw it? I suppose somebody did see it?'

'A coloured bloke. It was right into his front patch. Might settle for a new fence, but it could be dodgy.'

'Can you square up that end,' said Galloway, 'if we manage to get Roach off the hook job-wise?'

'Oh, come on, Roy. I'm not sticking my neck out for some drunken CID officer, and that's straight.'

'Hey, come on, Robert. Remember . . .'

Cryer's mouth twisted wryly. 'I'll do what I can. But I warn you, if it gets iffy – '

'Good boys can't be bad boys? How many favours have I done your firm in the past?' Galloway demanded. 'How many times have I got your lads out of the proverbial, hey?'

'And what am I doing here right this minute?' Cryer retorted. 'Look, I'm not arguing with you, Roy. I'm just telling you so you know where you stand. I'll go as far as I can, and that's it.'

He turned and went back down the stairs. Galloway pushed his way back into the room, scowling; then tried to wipe his features clean of anything but a respectful smile as Brownlow came in his direction, saying goodbye to the last stragglers.

'I think that went off rather well, don't you, Roy?'

'Not at all bad, guv.'

'Yes.' Brownlow looked past Galloway at the door, as if expecting to find something that ought not to be there and that would need dealing with in no uncertain manner. 'Well, home to the little woman, I suppose. Perhaps you'd pop in tomorrow morning, Roy. There are a few things I'd like to discuss.'

'Right, guv.'

As he moved at a leisurely pace to where June Ackland had finished washing up a batch of glasses, Brownlow raised a quizzical eyebrow. Quite adept with his eyebrows, was the chief super. 'Hanging on, are we, Roy?'

'Er . . . um . . . I just wanted to see WPC Ackland gets away safely, that's all.'

'Oh, yes,' said Brownlow archly. 'Well, good night, Roy. Ackland.'

'Good night, sir,' they said in chorus.

Galloway waited a few minutes until he was sure Brownlow was clear, then put out a hand. 'Right, give me those bottles.'

June opened her eyes wide in mock astonishment. 'So you're not taking me home, then, sir?'

'I thought Burnside had that in mind. He seemed to go off the boil though.'

'Yes,' said June reflectively. 'Funny, that. Not that I much fancied the idea, mind you.'

'I should hope not.'

'Funny,' she said again. 'I got some impression that somebody warned him off. Something about me being bespoken, as you might say. Viv Martella seemed to be getting a laugh out of it, anyway, but she wasn't going to tell me what was so funny.'

She handed the bottles over to him in a plastic bag.

'You certainly wouldn't want *me* to take you home, would

you?' said Galloway. 'I mean, some people might get the wrong idea.' He chuckled. 'Some might venture to think I'm this mystery man you're having it off with. And that would never do, would it?'

'No, perhaps you're right. It would never do.' She dried her hands, tugged her dress straight, and looked round for her raincoat. Her enticing little smile almost gave Galloway second thoughts; almost took his mind off the wonderful, exhilarating possibilities of those bottles in the plastic bag. But it was too late. 'I do have my reputation to think of,' said June. 'Don't I . . . *sir*?'

Fourteen

The piercing attack of the dentist's drill began to bite in an agonizing rhythm through his head. Only then it was no longer a drill but a skewer, screeching against his skull, torture without anaesthetic and without end. Ted Roach tried to fight it off. It only got worse, insistent, refusing to give up.

He opened his eyes. Bleak morning light splashed over an unfamiliar wall and a ceiling that was far too low. In the distance there was the throaty moan of a ship's siren. Much closer, his wristwatch alarm went bleeping on and on until he summoned up the energy and aim to cut it off.

There was blessed silence. Gradually the sounds of the outside world murmured their way into the cabin. A lorry trundled past, almost overhead. Somebody shouted something, his voice echoing between high walls.

Roach swung his legs off the bunk, sat up; and wished he hadn't.

He was still fully clothed, feeling sticky and rumpled and with a taste in his mouth which would have disgusted the least fastidious vulture. Blundering up on deck, he found the overcast sky far too bright. The uneven sheen along the wharf did nothing to help. Obviously there had been a steady drizzle overnight.

A truck splashed by and swung round the corner of one of the warehouses. Two hundred yards away a crane was starting to swing cargo aboard the freighter he had noticed the night before. The workers of the world were waking up and getting back on the job. Roach wished he could have postponed the whole business of waking up. He leaned against a wall until he could establish his balance. Cold bit into him. He thrust his hands in his pockets and tried to stop shivering.

A large lorry was drawn up behind a smaller van, tail to tail with only a small gap between them. Roach watched dully. Any minute now he had simply got to force himself to stand upright and walk away, back between those buildings and up the lanes to the main road; back, somehow or other, to Sun Hill and whatever was waiting for him there.

Two men came out from behind the van and stood talking by the cab. One of them laughed and rubbed his hands together, looking pleased rather than cold.

Now Roach was upright. He wiped his eyes, but the picture stayed clearly in focus. There was no mistake about it: the two men were Elkins and Crawley.

He made a cautious detour of the nearest warehouse and got a different angle down the lane. Framed in the opening was the open door of the van, partially masking the movements of a man reaching out to take something off another on the ground. It was a fair bet that sheepskin coats were involved in those movements.

Further along the row of warehouses was a phone box. Roach hugged the wall and made a dash for it.

The ringing tone seemed to go on for ever. Galloway surely couldn't have set off for the nick already – not after being kept late at that party? At last, just as he was about to hang up in despair, there came an answering snarl.

Roach said: 'Guv, I'm sorry to ring you at home at this hour, but – '

'Where the hell are you? Where've you been, you drunken berk? Do you realize just what you've let yourself in for?'

'Yes, all right, guv, all right. But listen. Elkins and Crawley. That's right. I've caught 'em red-handed. Coats and all, by the look of it. But we'll need some help.'

You could almost see Galloway dragging himself awake, scrambling out of bed in one of his killer moods, ready to organize the hunt and get going. Roach snapped out details and hung up so that the DI could start the round-up.

Now there was nothing to do for a while but wait.

Roach began to twitch with fear as the minutes ticked by – fear that the two men down there would be on their way, carrying all the evidence with them and spreading it through the markets before the Sun Hill lot could get here.

It was the most wonderful sight in the world, the Sierra nosing down the lane in search of him.

Galloway was first out. 'For your sake, Ted, I hope this isn't a load of old moody.'

'Look, I could have gone sick, missing – anything. I'm not asking for absolution, I'm just telling you. We've got a job. Believe me.'

'Let's have it, then. Where are they?'

'Down there. Right by those warehouse doors. They've got their van, they're liable to move off any time.'

Galloway led the way, with Roach limping behind him and Cryer, Mike Dashwood and Jimmy Carver crowding them as they turned the corner. There was a sudden shout, and someone ducked under the tail-bar of a lorry and was gone. Carver raced round the vehicle and took a few paces into the main storeroom beyond. There was nobody there.

Outside, Sergeant Cryer stood baffled. All at once there was nobody in sight except for themselves.

'They must be around here somewhere. In among those lorries at the end?'

'You go that way, Bob.' Galloway waved to Carver to come out of the gloomy interior. 'You go with Sergeant Cryer. Mike, come with me.'

Ted Roach gritted his teeth. They had been within his grasp – he had been so sure of them – they couldn't just slip away into nowhere like that.

Suddenly he was knocked to one side. Dashwood, stooping between two trucks, tripped and came lurching out. He put his arms round Roach and came to a halt.

'Not now, Dashers!'

'Stop messing about, Ted,' snapped Galloway. 'Are you never going to learn?'

'Oi, you lot.'

A man in a stained duffel coat came out of another door. He looked suspiciously at the three men in plain clothes, then with a touch more respect at Cryer and Carver.

'Good morning, sir.' Cryer saluted smartly.

'What are you lot doing round here?'

'Looking for two villains.' Galloway was not going to be left out of this. 'Wouldn't be working with you, would they, sir?'

The man looked him up and down. He had a large head with a large nose and a smile that might turn humorous or ferocious according to his mood. Probably he was good to work for if you didn't cross him.

'Two men just went into my cold store,' he said, 'as the fork-lift truck came out.'

Cryer took a quick glance along the line of buildings. 'Is there any other way out?'

'No,' The manager jabbed his thumb towards one heavy steel door, opening to let out a hazy white breath as two men humped something in and came hastily out. 'That's it.'

'All right if we go in there?'

'I wouldn't bother. They won't be in there very long. It's well below freezing.'

'Um.' Galloway pondered this a moment, watching a van backing up close to the door. 'Have your lads had their breakfast yet?'

'Not for another half hour.'

'They . . . er . . . they couldn't take an earlier one today, could they?'

An appreciative smile broadened on the manager's broad face. 'I don't see why not.'

'Right.' As the man went off to rejoin his work force, Galloway turned to Cryer. 'Now we've got that lot banged up in there, why don't we turn Ted's fiasco into a success story?'

'No chance,' said Roach. 'You don't think I'm fool enough to believe that this Elkins and Crawley saga is going to save my skin?'

Cryer began to move back towards the Sierra. 'Look, I've sweetened your Kingston ambassador for you. All you've got to do is straighten him out for a new fence, right?'

'O'Ryan's not a bad bloke, sarge,' Carver added.

'Come on, Ted.' Cryer bent towards the car door. 'I'll drop you off on the way back to the nick.'

Galloway was jolted into protest. 'What d'you mean, on the way back to the nick?'

'Well, the early shifts have got to relieve us. Look, I don't mind standing around here for the love of it. Might even get a bit of cod to take home to Shirley' – he glanced at the door to the cold store, now firmly shut – 'but you know the chief super and his views on overtime.'

'Don't you worry about the early turn or the overtime. I'll sort that out. With any luck that'll be the least of the chief super's worries.'

Cryer looked at him doubtfully. 'Have you got something up your sleeve, or what?'

Galloway smirked. 'I think you could say that.'

'All right. I'll take Ted over to O'Ryan's, and I'll be straight back.'

Now it was Roach's turn to protest. 'But I want to be around when – '

'On your way,' said Galloway.

'All right, guv.'

As Cryer and Roach drove off, Galloway turned to Mike Dashwood. 'On your toes to the golf club. See if you can trace where that Scotch has come from. If they're not open, wake them up. Me and Carver'll sit it out here. All right?'

'Yeah, all right.'

'And Mike . . . be discreet.'

Jimmy Carver began to pace up and down within a few yards of the cold store entrance, as if he mistrusted the security of the door. Roy Galloway took a stroll to the edge of the quay and looked out across the dark, oily water.

Carver had been right about one thing, anyway: O'Ryan was not at all a bad bloke. He greeted Sergeant Roach as a long-lost friend rather than as the dangerous drunk who had smashed up his front fence. There was coffee on the kitchen table, and the offer of breakfast. Roach could not take his eyes off the large bottle of tomato ketchup; and managed to still his stomach's querulous reaction and politely refuse anything in addition to the coffee.

Equally politely he asked Mr O'Ryan to let him know as soon as possible what repairs to the fence would cost. No trouble about an estimate – just make whatever arrangement suited him best with some local contractor, and Roach would be glad to let Mr O'Ryan have the money fast.

'Not Mr O'Ryan,' his host protested. 'Samuel. Sam to my friends.'

Samuel Winston O'Ryan did seem remarkably friendly, and extraordinarily uninterested in the splintered mess across his front garden. It took Roach's befuddled brain a little while to cotton on to the fact that the conversation kept leaning towards the subject of the special constabulary. Memories of those days of authority in Jamaica had never faded. Sam wanted to play his part again. His new friend Ted Roach must surely be able to get him into the special constabulary?

'Look, it's not what you know, it's who you know.' Roach stalled. 'You have to realize that.'

'But you can put in a good word for me, Mr Ted?'

'Well, I've got to put myself about a bit. You know, grease a few palms, you understand what I mean?'

'I'm with you, man.'

'See what we can do, anyway.'

'It is nice there is folk a man can rely on.'

'And now,' said Roach, 'what about this fence, then? When'll you be able to get it fixed and let me – '

'What fence, Mr Ted?' Samuel Winston O'Ryan propped his elbows on the table and beamed matily.

Mr Wiggins gave Mike Dashwood a far from cordial reception. The golf club car park was deserted, the cleaner had just arrived to go through the club room, and Wiggins had been expecting the usual slow crank-up to the day. Answering awkward questions was a thing to be avoided at the best of times. Awkward questions at this time in the morning were unheard of. But he listened numbly as Dashwood identified himself and intimated that some queries had arisen over local supplies of spirits to a number of local outlets. The word itself appeared to pain Mr Wiggins: this was a very select golf club, not an outlet.

Just how select and expensive, he was at pains to show the detective. Leading Dashwood through the cellars, he managed to exude the conviction that nobody lower than the rank of superintendent ought, strictly speaking, to be allowed into these hallowed vaults. They were indeed very smart, with dark timbers, an arched roof and rack upon rack of wine bottles. The wine was presumably genuine; the rest of the décor was fake, but very stylishly fake.

'It's not the wine we're concerned with, sir,' said Dashwood. 'It's mainly a matter of whisky.'

'Could you be a little more specific?'

'I'm sure you'll find it's just a routine enquiry, sir,' Dashwood soothed him. 'Just that these fake brands, they're becoming a bit of a problem.'

Wiggins flicked an imaginary speck off the cuff of his blazer. 'Fake brands?' he said indignantly. 'I can assure you that all our spirits are purchased through reputable merchants. We buy nothing over the counter. No cheap offers.'

'Then we should be able to wrap this up without having to bother you any further.'

'So I should hope.' Conceding an inch or two, Wiggins asked: 'Was there some particular brand that you have grounds for investigating?'

'Monroe County. It's a malt.'

'There's a coincidence. The Monroe bonded warehouse is down in Limehouse. One of our members is a manager of the company.'

'Quite a coincidence,' Dashwood agreed. He turned back towards the foot of the cellar steps. 'Shall we go back to your office, Mr Wiggins?'

'I thought you were looking for – '

'Perhaps you can show me a bottle in the bar. I'm sure you have one there?'

'But of course.' Wiggins ventured a prickly laugh. 'We're always getting asked for it. Mr . . .' He stopped himself.

'Mr . . .?' Dashwood prompted.

'I'm sorry. It's outrageous to even imagine that any produce supplied to us through the good offices of one of our members could be . . . might in any way be . . .'

They reached the bar, with Wiggins' office through a door behind it. A subdued light cast colourful glints on to and off the array of bottles.

Dashwood said: 'You've got a members' book? Addresses, dates of joining and all that?'

'Of course. But I can't imagine why you should want to see that.'

'Can I have a look at it?'

'No. Oh, no. Quite irregular.'

Dashwood put one hand on the bar and leaned on it. 'Mr Wiggins, this is a licensed bar, isn't it?'

'Of course.'

'Which comes under police supervision?'

Wiggins tried to preserve a stance of wounded dignity; then gave way.

Galloway and Jimmy Carver stood in the manager's office, looking out at the deserted quayside – deserted because all the men had disappeared into the hut at the end for their breakfast. Galloway fidgeted. He could just get an angle on the door of the cold store, but he was still worried.

'You sure there's not another way out?'

'Quite sure. And there's no way they can open that door: I've cut the electricity off at the end.'

Carver swayed. 'Do you think I could sit down, sir? I've been up all night.'

'Take a pew, son.' The manager shoved a chair forward. 'Would you gentlemen like a cup of coffee?'

Carver looked a shade more cheerful, but Galloway said:

'Don't get too comfortable there. You want to be out and about when they show themselves. Go and get a couple of those sheepskin coats. It must be brass monkeys in there.'

Reluctantly Carver left the office, just as Bob Cryer's car pulled in under the window.

'All set, then?' said the manager, patently looking forward to a bit of drama.

Galloway nodded. Time to go. The two of them went out and joined Cryer. Carver came tottering towards them, laden with sheepskin coats.

The manager gave a piercing whistle. One of his men drove a fork-lift truck towards them. 'All right, Fred. I'll do the driving. Just get that door open, will you?'

Well wrapped up, they clung on to the truck as the door swung back and they moved into the icy interior. Their bodies were warm enough, but the cold gnawed at their exposed faces. Gently the truck coasted along to the end of a huge four-tiered rack of food. It turned left and went along the end of the store while they peered down every aisle.

At last Cryer let out a whoop. 'There they are, the poor little buggers.'

Elkins and Crawley were huddled in a corner in search of warmth, or at least of something less cold. From their peaked expressions and the sound of their chattering teeth it did not appear that they were having much success.

'Now I know what they mean when they say "done up like a kipper",' observed Carver.

The truck slid in smoothly and stopped, blocking the way if the two men tried to make a run for it. Not that they showed much sign of being able to put one foot in front of the other.

Galloway leaned out from the truck. 'Could I interest you two gentlemen in a couple of bent sheepskin coats, eh?'

It was with considerable warmth, inside as well as outside, that they wheeled the wretched villains and the load of coats back to the nick. Half the men on duty took the chance of trying on the coats. 'Better than the old blue service, anyway.' Galloway watched indulgently. It was a good time. Knowing you'd got it right for once and sewn a whole case up neatly made you feel good. It had to. This would be one hell of a way to earn a living if you couldn't have the thrill of a triumph every now and then.

The door opened, and a chill swept through the room. Chief Superintendent Brownlow stood there for a moment; and it was a moment that cancelled out all the recent moments of pleasure.

'Inspector Galloway. I want to see you and Sergeant Roach in my office immediately.'

'I think Roach is out, sir. If there's anything I can – '

'Both of you,' said Brownlow. 'Immediately.'

The door slammed. Bob Cryer drew in a sad whistle. There was no mistaking the threat in the chief super's face. Galloway looked around the room, so silent all at once. Carver, too, had guessed, and looked sympathetic. Then there was Hollis . . .

And Galloway knew who had grassed. Hollis looked so innocent, not knowing anything that had happened or why the depression had fallen so suddenly on everyone else. But not nearly innocent enough. There was just that one telltale flicker of a self-satisfied grimace.

Galloway pushed past him and out into the corridor. June Ackland seemed to be having trouble with a stray dog. He said, 'When you've stopped messing about with that dog, get Sergeant Roach back here now. On the double.'

'He's back already, sir. Just gone up to the canteen. Oh, and sir' – as Galloway swung away – 'thank you for taking me home last night, sir.'

Galloway pounded up the stairs and lifted a finger to Ted Roach. Nobody seemed to need words any more. It was all in the air: Roach got to his feet, knowing what was about to hit him, and miserably plodded along behind his boss to the door of Brownlow's office.

The chief super had been building up a head of steam while he waited for them. The door was barely closed behind them when he blasted it all out.

'Your conduct last night, Roach, was unbecoming to any police officer, let alone a detective sergeant. It was a disgrace.

Not only to the police force in general but to myself in particular.'

'Sir.'

'I took great exception to your vulgar behaviour at the party. An appalling exhibition, in front of my guests. But far worse than that, Roach, when you left the party you were in no state to drive a motor vehicle. It was obvious to everybody there that you had had too much to drink. And as for you, Inspector Galloway, standing by and allowing him to – '

'Sir, I must – '

'I shall be glad if you do not interrupt, inspector.' The intercom on his desk chose this moment to bleep a signal at him. He leaned angrily forward. 'I gave instructions that I was not to be disturbed.'

'It's for DI Galloway, sir.' It was June Ackland's voice. 'Says it's very urgent.'

Brownlow hesitated, then nodded at the handset. 'All right. Take it there. But it had *better* be urgent.' He sat back, fuming.

In the receiver Dashwood said: 'Guv, I've traced the Scotch connection. Sorry it took so long, but I've been going through the club's spirit receipts for the last quarter.'

'And . . .?'

'And Richie Dicks, one of the chief super's guests last night, he's a manager of Monroe's bonded warehouse. Do you want me to go and pick him up?'

'What's the rest of it?'

'Sounds like a straight theft. Employee theft. He probably considers it one of the perks of the job. You know, lifting a couple of bottles now and again. Know what I mean?'

Galloway took a deep breath and tried to avoid the chief super's menacing stare. 'Don't,' he said forcefully. 'I repeat, *don't* take this matter any further.'

'But guv – '

'Return to the station, Dashwood, and we'll talk about it here. All right?'

'I'll be with you in about fifteen minutes. See you, guv.'

'Cheers.' And it was with dawning good cheer that Galloway

now met Brownlow's gaze. 'A matter of great delicacy's come up, sir. I think we ought to talk alone. Could you leave us, Ted?'

'Inspector Galloway, I have not finished with Sergeant Roach yet.'

'No, sir. But just for a minute or two, could I have a word? Between ourselves.'

Ted Roach escaped. Brownlow watched him go with great displeasure. 'What are you up to, Galloway?'

'Last night, sir,' said Galloway, 'a Mr Richie Dicks, a guest of yours from the golf club, knowingly brought stolen bottles of Scotch to the party.'

Bob Cryer paced up and down the front office. Ted Roach watched him guiltily. It was long past Bob's time to knock off and go home, and after last night's party and this morning's burst of activity he looked dead tired. But like the rest of them he was hanging on, waiting to find out what had happened, hoping for a miracle.

Roach had given up hoping for a miracle. He'd had his promotion now. This was the end. All those wasted years studying. Or maybe that wasn't where the waste had been. Last night . . .

He had been remorseful so many times, the morning after. A fat lot of good it had been.

Hollis crossed the office almost on tiptoe. He was almost out of the door when Cryer said: 'You got in mighty early this morning, Hollis?'

'Couldn't sleep, sarge.'

'Guilty conscience?'

'Not me, sarge. *I've* got nothing to feel guilty about. Just that after that party, you know how it is . . . maybe something I ate.'

'Remembered to thank the chief super for his hospitality, did you?'

'Well, I did see him soon after I got in, sarge – '

'And had a word or two?'

Roach got the drift of it all right. He wanted to chuck himself right across the table between them and hammer the living bloody daylights out of that little creep. But he was in enough trouble already.

'Only in the line of duty,' Hollis was saying unctuously. 'You know, sarge, keeping my eyes open so I'll know how to cope when I get round to taking the new job over full-time.'

He was going to be a right one, was Reg Hollis: oh, a worthy successor to Henry Talbot. In spite of all the dangers, Roach felt tempted to go out in a blaze of glory by crushing that slimy face against the wall. Fortunately, or unfortunately, Hollis had gone.

It would have been a blaze of glory, too. Each and every one of the rest of them would have been on his side. He would at least have left them a happy memory to talk about for years to come. Leaving them . . . it was something he had not yet faced up to. Leaving them and missing the whole shower of them. Mike Dashwood and his infuriating habits, the bloody woodentops mucking things up over and over again . . . and now look at them, worrying much more about him than he had any right to expect.

It was the drink still making him maudlin. So he told himself, without believing it.

'Why don't you go home, sarge?' June Ackland asked Cryer quietly. 'You're dead beat.'

'I want to wait and see what's happened.'

'Well, I only hope when I'm in trouble, God forbid, that you'll be waiting in the wings ready to bail me out.'

Ted Roach could stand no more down here. He trailed off towards the stairs and the CID offices, knowing they would be watching him go and talking about him in muted tones.

Bloody woodentops.

Mike Dashwood was trying to swat a fly with a rolled-up newspaper.

'Stop prancing up and down,' growled Roach. 'You make me feel worse.'

Dashwood threw the paper in the waste basket. 'Are you sure it wasn't too late?'

'What?' So far as Roach was concerned, everything was too late.

'My phone call.'

'I wish I'd known about that stolen Scotch. I'm telling you, there'd have been no waiting around till the morning. I would well and truly have nicked Mr Dickie Dicks. Or I'd have been out there first thing, wheeling him in.'

'Then the guv'nor wouldn't have had anything to trade with, would he?' Dashwood pointed out.

Roach was not counting on much of a reward from that trade. Brownlow was ready to have him hung, drawn and quartered: there had been this brief reprieve, but any minute now he would be back in the office getting his final comeuppance. He knew it.

'That bloody retirement party,' he moaned. 'And all for someone I never could stand anyway. Should never have let myself be pressurized. Should have stuck to my principles and refused. Never again.'

The door opened with a swirl of air which lifted papers from the desk. Galloway was in the room, moving fast and pushy, his usual self, full of himself. 'Grab your coat, Mike. We're going for a meal.'

'We are?'

'Chief super says so. Orders. Take a break, have a meal.'

Roach, incredulous, watched them turning back towards the open door. 'What's happening? What about me?'

'Didn't think you'd be interested,' said Galloway with a mocking sideways glance. 'Knowing how you hate being pressurized.'

They had paused and were waiting for him. Dashwood was laughing for no obvious reason other than sheer pleasure. Galloway tried to suppress his own grin of triumph.

Roach, shaky on his feet, tried to match Galloway's tone of voice. 'Well, if the chief super says you've got to go some place, you've got to go, haven't you?'

They made their way downstairs. Sergeant Cryer took one look, said nothing, and finally went home tired but content.